"As long as you [...] done." Fotis turned away without waiting for an answer.

Obey! "There's just one thing," Rosamund murmured. "You didn't ask if *I* had any ground rules."

Satisfaction was a pleasing glow as those broad shoulders stiffened.

"And you have ground rules, of course."

His tone spoke of barely contained patience. What was he expecting? A request that they detour so she could shop for designer handbags? A demand for vintage champagne in the limo?

"Just one." Rosamund waited long enough for him to raise his eyebrows at the delay. Good. She had his full attention. "Courtesy, Mr. Mavridis. It's non-negotiable. You might be in charge, as you so succinctly put it, but I expect to be consulted, not ordered. Besides, if we want the public to believe you're my companion rather than my bodyguard, you'll need to practice politeness, with me and the people we meet."

"And you'll reciprocate?"

Rosamund picked up her bag and straightened her jacket. "Of course. Haven't you noticed?" She moved past him towards the door. "If I weren't polite I'd have already mentioned you're the most arrogant, objectionable man I've met in a long time."

Annie West has devoted her life to an intensive study of charismatic heroes who cause the best kind of trouble for their heroines. As a sideline she researches locations for romance whenever she can, from vibrant cities to desert encampments and fairy-tale castles. Annie lives in eastern Australia with her hero husband, between sandy beaches and gorgeous wine country. She finds writing the perfect excuse to postpone housework. To contact her or join her newsletter, visit annie-west.com.

Books by Annie West

Harlequin Presents

The Desert King Meets His Match
Reclaiming His Runaway Cinderella
Reunited by the Greek's Baby
The Housekeeper and the Brooding Billionaire
Nine Months to Save Their Marriage
His Last-Minute Desert Queen
A Pregnancy Bombshell to Bind Them
Signed, Sealed, Married
Unknown Royal Baby
Ring for an Heir
Queen by Royal Command
Stolen Pregnant Bride

Visit the Author Profile page
at Harlequin.com for more titles.

FORBIDDEN PRINCESS'S BILLIONAIRE BODYGUARD

ANNIE WEST

PRESENTS

If you purchased this book without a cover you should be aware that this book is stolen property. It was reported as "unsold and destroyed" to the publisher, and neither the author nor the publisher has received any payment for this "stripped book."

Recycling programs for this product may not exist in your area.

ISBN-13: 978-1-335-21346-4

Forbidden Princess's Billionaire Bodyguard

Copyright © 2025 by Annie West

All rights reserved. No part of this book may be used or reproduced in any manner whatsoever without written permission.

Without limiting the exclusive rights of any author, contributor or the publisher of this publication, any unauthorized use of this publication to train generative artificial intelligence (AI) technologies is expressly prohibited. Harlequin also exercises their rights under Article 4(3) of the Digital Single Market Directive 2019/790 and expressly reserves this publication from the text and data mining exception.

This is a work of fiction. Names, characters, places and incidents are either the product of the author's imagination or are used fictitiously. Any resemblance to actual persons, living or dead, businesses, companies, events or locales is entirely coincidental.

For questions and comments about the quality of this book, please contact us at CustomerService@Harlequin.com.

TM and ® are trademarks of Harlequin Enterprises ULC.

Harlequin Enterprises ULC
22 Adelaide St. West, 41st Floor
Toronto, Ontario M5H 4E3, Canada
www.Harlequin.com

HarperCollins Publishers
Macken House, 39/40 Mayor Street Upper,
Dublin 1, D01 C9W8, Ireland
www.HarperCollins.com

Printed in Lithuania

FORBIDDEN PRINCESS'S BILLIONAIRE BODYGUARD

This book is dedicated to the wonderful Mr. West,
who listens to me ramble about plots and characters,
who is there through thick and thin,
who *always* cheers me on, and
who builds me bookcases!
Happy sighs.

CHAPTER ONE

ROSAMUND SCANNED THE STUDY, antique bookcases rising to a frescoed ceiling. Up there haughty gods stared down at her from puffy clouds. She didn't need to look up to know how disdainfully they frowned at her. This had been her father's study. She'd spent too many hours here being told the many ways she didn't measure up.

She'd reminded him too much of her mother, more interested in people than rules. But her father was gone. Now it was her half-brother sitting behind the royal desk.

She turned to meet eyes so like their father's that for a second she was flung back to the last time she'd seen the old king. Even on his deathbed there'd been no rapprochement, despite her attempts. Any faint hope that he had, at some level, loved her, had shrivelled.

She should have known better.

Rosamund blinked. Leon's eyes were the same colour but he didn't wear their father's habitual scowl.

She saw shadows beneath his eyes that spoke of tiredness, and reined in her impatience.

'Leon, I've already explained I can't have a security detail from the palace.'

'Can't or won't?' His frustration was clear. 'It would be a temporary measure only.'

That was what her father had said when she was seventeen, yet the situation had lasted until she was twenty-one, legally an adult, and finally able to refuse it.

Four years of having not just a single discreet guard but a group of burly, hatchet-jawed men who were as unobtrusive as a diamond tiara in a dole queue. They'd shadowed her so closely she'd had no private space. No wonder they'd scared off even her friends.

Which had been the idea. After the scandal her father hadn't focused on keeping her safe but ensuring she didn't embarrass him again. She'd naively fallen for a charming, handsome man only to learn he just wanted her as a stepping stone to power. When she ended things he'd retaliated, leaking salacious stories to the press with damning photos, some not even of her but carefully doctored.

That didn't matter to the king. She'd damaged the royal family's reputation. He'd never forgiven her.

Her skin prickled at the humiliating memories. Of being continually surrounded by men who treated her like a prisoner rather than someone needing protection. It had been a very public, very deliberate punishment.

'It's not feasible. I have an aversion to oversized thugs being privy to my personal life.'

'If you're averse to thugs, you shouldn't have got mixed up with Brad Ricardo.'

Rosamund rolled her eyes. She'd tried to explain she wasn't mixed up with the man, but no one wanted to listen. She should have known better than to try. The palace never listened.

'I have no intention of seeing him again.'

'He might have other plans. You don't think a man like that might view you as unfinished business?'

Not in the way everyone thinks!

She remembered Ricardo's eyes when he realised what she'd done. That dark stare had been like a honed blade, threatening to eviscerate her.

That night she'd acted on impulse but she couldn't regret her actions. She'd met people like him before, so engrossed in their own needs they'd take advantage of anyone who got in their way.

'He and I aren't even on the same continent. I've got no plans to return to the States soon.'

This time the silence held a different quality. Not mere frustration but something that made her nape prickle.

'Leon, what aren't you telling me?'

'He's threatened you, and a man like him has a long reach. He has contacts in Europe.'

Her stomach curdled. She'd told herself his threat had been bluster but never quite believed it. That was why she'd abruptly ended her American stay.

'You're saying he's dangerous? Physically dangerous?'

There was a pause as if he decided how much to tell her. 'Talk to me, Leon. I have a right to know.'

'The authorities in America are investigating him.'

Rosamund sank back in her chair, a shiver working its way down her backbone. She'd known the man was poison, but a criminal? 'For what crimes?'

'Embezzlement and assault.'

Her shiver became a shudder and she wrapped her arms around her middle. Embezzlement didn't surprise her. She'd seen how plausible and charming he could be in pursuit of money. As for assault…she'd told herself that malevolent stare he'd given her didn't matter. Now she wondered.

'How bad was the assault?'

Leon looked grim. 'Bad.'

Rosamund opened her mouth to ask for details then decided she didn't want to know. 'If the police are investigating, Ricardo will have more on his mind than me.'

Her half-brother wasn't convinced. 'The assault charge won't proceed. The victim refuses to testify for fear of reprisal.'

A lead weight dropped in her stomach. She'd known Ricardo was bad news, but this...

Leon pressed on, his expression stern. 'Ricardo doesn't yet know about the big embezzlement investigation. If they prove the case he'll be imprisoned for years. Your protection would be for a short time while the police investigate. After that, hopefully he won't be a problem to anyone.'

It seemed far-fetched that the man could harm her in Europe. But she couldn't forget that venomous look, the blood-chilling words he'd spat at her.

'How short a time?'

'A week or two.'

Rosamund shook her head. 'I've got important public engagements coming up.'

Engagements she couldn't attend with a mob of the palace's anything-but-discreet minders surrounding her. It would make a mockery of the events and detract from their purpose.

Her chest squeezed. Being guest of honour at the festival to honour her mother's remarkable career would be a double-edged sword, a proud moment and an emotional trial. But she *had* to attend.

The world had known Juliette Bernard as a gifted actor before she married a king. To Rosamund she was the one person who'd loved her unconditionally. She'd been her role model, a beacon of warmth against the king's cold, judgemental presence.

'I know you have engagements, Rosa.' Leon's use of the

rare diminutive surprised her. As did the unfamiliar note almost of apology in his voice.

She tried to recall when he'd last called her that. When she was a little girl, she supposed.

She didn't loathe Leon as she had their father. They simply led separate lives. In fact they didn't really know each other. Leon was so much older, the son of the king's first wife, so that when Rosamund was born he'd been away at boarding school.

Now he lived in Cardona's royal palace while she had an apartment on the far side of the city. But for the last several years, while their father was alive, she'd spent more time out of the country than in it and Leon was always busy with royal duties which usually didn't involve her.

'I know how important the festival is to you. That's why I'm not suggesting you cancel, though you'd be safer here.'

She stiffened, gripping the arms of her chair. Her father had been dictatorial enough to prevent her leaving the kingdom on at least one occasion. 'Go on.'

'I'm offering a compromise. Instead of a close protection team from the palace, you'll have one companion. Not an official bodyguard but someone I trust and know can keep you safe.'

She stared suspiciously. '*Not* a bodyguard?'

'Definitely not. He's a businessman these days, but he has the necessary skills to keep danger at bay.'

Rosamund's eyebrows rose. 'Some businessman. What does he do, run a karate school?'

Leon's lips twitched. 'He's more of a policy advisor.'

She knew the type. She'd seen them with their briefcases and frowns, buzzing around the royal offices. Yet he must be more than that for Leon to suggest him. She was about to ask for more detail when something clicked.

'You've already arranged this, haven't you? Without asking me.'

Leon shrugged and spread his hands. 'You refused a security team when my secretary contacted you. But I can't let you go without *any* protection.'

She frowned. Her father had washed his hands of her. It felt odd to have someone watch out for her. 'That's a lot of trouble to go to, locating someone able to blend in *and* intervene if there's trouble.'

Serious eyes met hers and she felt a dart of shock as she read Leon's concern. 'I don't want you hurt, Rosa. You're my sister.'

A lump lodged in her throat. He wasn't worried about the outcry if something happened to a member of the royal family. He was concerned for *her*. *His sister*, not merely his obligation. It wasn't what she'd expected when she'd been summoned to the palace.

She'd barely ever spent time alone with Leon. She wasn't used to tenderness from her family, not since her mother died years before.

'I...' She cleared her throat. 'What arrangements have you made?'

Seeing relief spread across his features, Rosamund knew she'd accept his plan. He'd taken the trouble to find a compromise she could live with. That was unprecedented. The palace never compromised. And he'd done it because he cared.

She silently vowed that when she returned to Cardona, she'd spend some time with the brother she barely knew.

'He'll meet you off the plane in Paris. There's just one condition.'

'Go on, I'm game. What is it?'

'The only way he can reasonably be by your side all the

time without appearing like the bodyguards you detest. As far as the public's concerned, you're a couple. That will explain why he's at your side at every event. Just don't say anything to dispel the idea and there'll be no questions raised.'

A pretend lover? 'But—'

'That's the deal, Rosa. You've got no idea how difficult this was to organise. But he's agreed, on condition he calls the shots. Any hint of danger and he's in charge.' The warmth she'd seen in Leon's expression vanished, leaving him looking almost as stern as their father. 'So, Rosamund, will you take it or leave it?'

You should have left it. You should have said no and walked straight out the door. He wouldn't have barred you from leaving the country. Probably.

But regrets were pointless. She was almost there. Far below, she saw the sprawl that was Paris. Leon had loaned her the king's private jet. The main thing was that she'd be at the event as promised.

That was what she had to concentrate on.

Not the way all her plans had been disrupted.

She'd been on her way to the airport when she learned her Paris hotel booking had been cancelled. Ditto the car she'd rented to drive south when the Paris events were over.

Then, after rushing to be at the airport by the revised deadline, she'd discovered the earlier departure time wasn't because Leon needed the plane but because his bodyguard-who-wasn't-a-bodyguard had decided she needed to arrive in Paris early.

Without consulting her. About anything! He'd just decreed and somehow everything had changed.

Rosamund chewed her lip, banking down fury at the man's high-handedness. If this was how he operated, they were going to clash. Despite her father's view of her, she wasn't flighty or stupid, and she appreciated common decency. Like a request and an explanation. Not finding out after the fact that everything had been altered.

Fotis Mavridis clearly didn't believe in consultation.

It irked her that in the little time she'd spent researching him she'd found virtually nothing. He was Greek. He ran a company called Mystikos, which she learned was Greek for secret or hidden. The word was annoyingly apt because though she'd found a few sparse references to it providing advice to various governments, she couldn't find the company website or details of its business.

As for Fotis Mavridis, he could almost be a figment of her brother's imagination. There were no photos, few biographical details, almost nothing to indicate what sort of man she was about to meet.

Apart from bossy, rude and, by definition, unlikable.

She thought of the policy advisors she'd met. They led sedentary, office-bound lives. It was hard to imagine one of them protecting her should Ricardo try to get even with her for disrupting his plans.

Her mouth twisted wryly as she tried to imagine a balding bureaucrat standing between her and danger, his agitated breaths straining his shirt across a podgy stomach.

There must be more to this man than Leon's description suggested.

The jet landed and taxied to the edge of the private airfield. There was a bustle at the door as steps were put in position.

Rosamund was reaching for the shoes she'd slipped off when her skin prickled. The atmosphere changed, becoming charged, like at the onset of an electrical storm.

She looked up, and up further. Dimly she was aware of

her pulse thudding a quickened beat. Of a spasm low in her body and her nipples peaking, abrading her bra.

All that in a millisecond as she took in the stranger before her.

His shoulders were straight and wide under his black leather jacket. There were black jeans too and a dark T-shirt that hinted at a steel-toned body. Black-as-night hair, winged ebony eyebrows and a dusting of midnight stubble on his hard-hewn jaw. But shockingly his eyes were light. They reminded her of the sea, a mix of blue and green and maybe even gold, as if the sun glittered over liquid depths.

With his strong features—she couldn't call him handsome but arresting—Rosamund could imagine him cast as a fallen angel. Not just any fallen angel. With his incredible presence he had to be Lucifer, their leader.

Maybe those eyes were a reminder of those glory days before he was kicked out of heaven. Rosamund had never seen anything like that colour which, even as she watched, seemed to glow more golden.

Something shuddered inside her. Something shockingly like recognition. Awareness.

Nonsense! The artist in her simply wondered how to capture that precise shade.

'Princess Rosamund.'

It wasn't a question but a flat statement of certainty. Yet it was more too. In just five syllables his softly modulated baritone conveyed disdain. Scorn, even.

Suddenly, shockingly, she knew who this man must be and discovered she'd walked into a nightmare.

This was the man sent to protect her? Who'd act as her partner for the duration of the trip?

Disbelief and dismay filled her. Despite his arrogance and his contempt, it would be easy for a woman to find him attractive. To want to put her hands on him, test that tensile strength and try to learn the secrets of his body.

No wonder every instinct screamed a warning.

It was impossible to sit under that scorching scrutiny.

Ignoring her shoes she rose, standing tall and cloaking herself in the illusion of confidence as her mother had taught her. She'd never been more grateful for those early lessons.

'*Kyrie Mavridis. Kalimera.*' She inclined her head as if graciously accepting a compliment and felt a flicker of satisfaction at his momentary surprise.

'You speak Greek?'

Clearly he hadn't expected that and she dearly wished she could claim that advantage. She suspected she'd need every advantage she could muster to deal with this man who was *not* like any policy advisor she'd seen. So much for a balding, paunchy bureaucrat. She'd have words with Leon when she returned. He should have warned her.

'Alas, no. Just a few pleasantries.'

She paused, far too aware of their height difference now they stood toe-to-toe. She rarely wore high heels and wished she'd worn some on the plane. As it was, barefoot she had to tilt her head to meet his eyes.

He inclined his head, his unsmiling mouth betraying no pleasure in her company.

What was the man's problem? Couldn't he even pretend to the usual social niceties?

It intrigued her that Leon had managed to persuade this man who looked as persuadable as a block of basalt, into looking out for her.

Did he owe Leon some debt?

'You're ready to go?' His tone was brusque.

'In a moment.' His eagerness to be gone and his refusal to play nice spurred her to take her time, letting down her hair then gathering it up, winding it around her hand and fixing it more securely. Only when she was satisfied it would pass muster for any paparazzi did she turn to accept her jacket, held out to her by the steward. She gave a man a warm smile. 'Thank you very much, Philippe.'

Then her shoes. She slipped them on, wishing the heels were three times the height.

She was reaching for her shoulder bag when her Greek minder said, 'I came on-board to discuss the ground rules before this goes any further.'

Rosamund's eyebrows lifted. She'd promised Leon she'd be discreet about this arrangement. It seemed Fotis Mavridis hadn't got that memo. Or, she realised as she met that challenging stare, he had his own priorities. Any thought that he was dependent on her half-brother vanished.

'Thank you, Philippe.' She nodded at the steward. 'We'll follow you out in a moment.'

When the cabin was empty she gestured to the empty seats. 'Shall we sit while we talk?'

'That won't be necessary. This won't take long.'

His voice was uninflected, his stare blank, but she knew it hid disapproval if not dislike. She had enough experience to know.

Once, long ago, that would have hurt, to be judged and found wanting for no good reason. But she wasn't naïve anymore. She was a woman who got on with her life, forging her own path. If she allowed herself to be upset by negative opinions, she'd be a hermit.

Even so, she was tempted to sink back into her seat and let him stand there, alone. Except she'd get a crick in her neck and he'd probably enjoy looming over her.

'So. Ground rules.' She smiled encouragingly as if unaware of the negative energy thrumming off him. 'Please continue.'

For a heartbeat she sensed curiosity behind the mask. 'Actually, there's only one. I'm in charge. What I say goes, otherwise the deal's off.'

'In charge of what, precisely? Countering any physical threat? Believe me, I'm happy to leave that to you.'

Any thought that he mightn't be up to the task had disintegrated. He radiated competence and though his stance was easy, there was a restrained power about him that made her think he could handle any threat.

'In charge of you.' He paused to let that sink in. '*I* decide where you go. When and how you go and where you stay. Any problem with that and I'm out.'

He talked to her as if she were a six-year-old, not a twenty-eight-year-old who'd made her own way in the world for a long time. Not like a client. Or a royal, for that matter.

Indignation rose and a burning desire to tell this man where he could get off.

But Leon would immediately replace the man with a team of bodyguards, despite her wishes. Besides, she was curious. She was used to people who didn't know her judging her, but this felt different.

Why? They hadn't met before. There was no way she'd have forgotten this man. Maybe he didn't like royals. Or women. She shook off the notion this was personal. That wasn't possible.

'So,' he said with a telling curl of his lips, 'if you're going to opt out, now's the time.'

That's what he wants. For you to end the deal and walk away. Why?

The temptation to agree was strong. She didn't like her instant and all-consuming awareness of him. She didn't like *him*. She'd prefer not to see him again. But that was what he wanted. Why else stomp in here and bark out his ultimatum?

Okay, okay. So he doesn't bark. He doesn't raise his voice. In fact the sound of that deep baritone voice, so soft it whispers across your skin, is ridiculously appealing.

Rosamund drew a slow breath, ignoring the regrettable things that voice did to her hormones. She could play into his hands but all that would achieve was her lumbered with the team of security guards she'd already rejected.

'Opt out?' She looked up with wide eyes that belied the welter of anger and indignation churning in her stomach. 'I was told you'd protect me from threat. If you're able to do that I'm grateful.'

What she was *actually* grateful for was that her mother had been an esteemed actress. She'd learnt from the best how to conceal her thoughts, how to project the emotions she chose, no matter what she felt.

She saw the flicker of something cross his features. Surprise? Disappointment?

'I understand you're the expert on my safety.' No matter how galling that was. 'I note you've already come up with alternative plans for my accommodation and transport. Perhaps that was because it's better not to signal in advance where I'm staying and how I'm travelling?'

For the longest time he said nothing but finally he nodded curtly. 'Yes.'

See, that wasn't so hard was it?

She stifled the temptation to say it aloud. No point prodding the bear.

Except, while she might have learnt to put pragmatism before pride, she had her limits. It didn't take a genius to know this man would test those limits to the full.

Besides, if the bear deserved prodding…

'As long as you can get me to the events I'm scheduled to attend, and the people I need to see, that's fine.'

She smiled benignly. *That's what your job is after all.* But she kept her lips closed.

His scrutiny intensified, those uniquely coloured eyes regarding her with a laser focus that scraped her skin.

Annoying man, but clever. He knows there's something going on behind the smile.

That made two of them. She could almost hear the wheels turning in that arrogant head of his.

'So, are we done here, Mr Mavridis?'

He nodded. 'As long as you'll obey me, we're done.' He turned away without waiting for an answer.

Obey! 'There's just one thing,' she murmured. 'You didn't ask if *I* had any ground rules.'

Satisfaction was a pleasing glow as those broad shoulders stiffened. She wondered if he'd pretend he hadn't heard and simply walk away. But slowly he turned.

'And you have ground rules, of course.'

He didn't grimace but his tone spoke of barely contained patience. What was he expecting? A request that they detour so she could shop for designer handbags? A demand for vintage champagne in the limo? A coy request that they not get too close when they pretended to be a couple in public?

As if she had any fears on that score! Whatever this man's weakness was, it wasn't her. He looked like he could barely stand her presence.

What a relief.

'Just one.' Rosamond waited long enough for him to raise his eyebrows at the delay. Good. She had his full attention. 'Courtesy, Mr Mavridis. It's non-negotiable. You might be in charge, as you so succinctly put it, but I expect to be consulted, not ordered. You might not think much of life's little courtesies. Greetings, please and thank you. But most people prefer to be treated with respect. I'm one of them.

'Besides, if we want the public to believe you're my companion rather than my bodyguard, you'll need to practise politeness, with me and the people we meet.'

'And you'll reciprocate?'

Rosamund picked up her bag and straightened her jacket. 'Of course. Haven't you noticed?' She moved past him towards the door. 'If I weren't polite I'd have already mentioned you're the most arrogant, objectionable man I've met in a long time.' She paused to look over her shoulder into his narrowed stare. 'Shall we go?'

CHAPTER TWO

Fotis frowned, replaying her parting words at the plane.

Not that he wanted to be amused, or impressed. But Princess Rosamund of Cardona had surprised him.

That was unusual. He made it his business to be prepared. Yet from the moment he'd boarded the royal jet everything had been out of kilter.

It wasn't a sensation he liked. He'd spent a lifetime ensuring he was in control of his world, not the other way around. His mouth flattened as he watched the Parisian streets go by.

In his peripheral vision he saw her, busy on her phone. She hadn't looked at him since they'd climbed into the back of the limo. Such complete disregard was deliberate.

Like the way she'd sashayed down the plane's steps. She hadn't wriggled her hips or tossed her head. Oh no, she was too regal for that, but the proud set of her shoulders and her absolute composure proclaimed nothing he'd done or said fazed her. He was beneath her notice.

For a millisecond he considered doing something that would *really* ruffle her feathers.

On the plane she'd casually let down her hair then redone it, just to make the point that *she* set the timetable. What would she do if he reached out now and tugged it undone, threading his fingers through the shining tresses, dragging her head back so her throat and mouth were vulnerable to him?

The idea was tempting even for a man who didn't allow himself to be provoked. Who did *not* manhandle women.

Admittedly she'd had a point. He'd ditched social niceties. How that must have shocked a woman used to smarm and charm and getting her own way.

It was a timely reminder of who and what she was.

This was the last place he'd be if he hadn't been virtually blackmailed into it. He despised her, with good reason. He knew her sort intimately. Usually he ignored them, but when others suffered it was different.

Inevitably pain resonated as he thought of Nico.

His little brother had died because Fotis had failed to protect him. And because their mother had been too absorbed in seducing a rich new lover to care for her children. She was another shallow, self-absorbed woman, used to getting what she wanted.

Yet despite his hatred of vain socialites, he lingered on the memory of Princess Rosamund's hair settling over the upper slopes of her peaked breasts. She'd worn a silky camisole the colour of mountain violets that clung enough to reveal as much as it concealed.

To his chagrin he'd imagined cupping those breasts and feeling her pebbled nipples against his palms.

Cursing under his breath, he dragged out his phone. He might have been corralled into looking after a spoilt madam but that didn't mean he'd neglect his own business.

The car slowed and Rosamund looked up from her email as it swung off the quiet street and into a private garage. The street wasn't familiar and she didn't even know which *ar-*

rondissement of Paris they'd entered. She'd been too busy trying to ignore her dour companion to keep track of the city.

She turned to ask their location but he'd already exited the vehicle. So had the driver. She put her phone away and gathered her bag, by which time the driver was holding her open door.

'Thank you.' She smiled and received the tiniest nod in response. Had his boss ordered him not to get friendly? Or for some reason did he, like Fotis Mavridis, view her as the enemy?

She told herself her imagination was running away with her, something her father had often complained about. Yet she didn't need to be clairvoyant to know Mavridis really didn't want anything to do with her. What *was* his problem?

She moved away from the car, noting the garage door had shut behind them with a soft thud. It was sensible, bringing her somewhere she wouldn't be seen alighting from the vehicle in the street.

Mavridis knew what he was doing. With the limo's tinted windows no one had seen her in the traffic. No one knew her location unless they'd followed from the airport.

For a shockingly claustrophobic moment, standing in the dimly lit garage at an unknown location, brought by men she didn't know, fear spidered across her skin, drawing it tight. Her pulse thudded in her throat. Even Leon didn't know where she was.

Tension roiled in her stomach and she felt a sickeningly abrupt rush of adrenaline. She made herself exhale slowly, short breath in and a longer one out. She loosened her jaw, dropped her shoulders and felt her heartbeat slow.

Then she noticed her unwilling bodyguard in an open doorway, light spilling from behind him. With his face in shadow it was impossible to read his expression. Had he noticed the way her hand had crept into her shoulder bag to clutch her phone?

She made herself walk towards him across the bare cement floor. She'd almost reached him when he turned and walked away.

His lack of manners was a slap in the face. That intrigued her for, though she was a princess, in daily life she didn't live as one. She did her share of royal events but instead of living in the palace, had her own apartment. She didn't get the red carpet treatment except at official events. Friends and work associates called her by her first name, never her title.

But he'd been employed to look after a princess. For all he knew, her royal position was her full-time job. Turning his back wasn't polite for anyone, but with royalty it was a damning insult. Was that why he'd done it?

Rosamund mulled that over as she followed him down a hall. He wasn't to know that far from revelling in her royal birthright, she'd always craved a normal life. Aristocratic privilege wasn't all it was cracked up to be.

It was tempting to tell him he'd have to try harder with his insults. But why bother? He was a necessary encumbrance for a short period. The less time she wasted thinking about him the better.

Yeah, right. After you spent the whole car ride reading the same page in the new contract. Just because Mr Macho Grumpy was beside you, taking up all the oxygen.

He hadn't spoken. Hadn't looked her way. But his presence had overwhelmed her.

Rosamund didn't do overwhelmed. She didn't give any man power over her. It had been a hard-won lesson but one she'd committed to heart.

'Where are we?' she said as she followed him into a big,

sunny kitchen that looked onto a surprisingly large and inviting garden.

'The house where we'll stay while you're in Paris.'

'You rented a whole house?'

She'd only seen the massive garage, a marble-floored hallway and this state-of-the-art kitchen. But that was enough to know this was no ordinary house.

'You think your brother can't afford it?'

She plonked her bag on the island bench that looked bigger than the average kitchen, then planted her palms on the cool stone. 'I pay my own way. I'm not here at the state's expense. Usually I stay in a hotel.'

Did she imagine a flicker of surprise in his eyes? 'This is more secure.' After a moment he added, 'Don't worry, I don't expect you to pay. It's not a rental.'

Slowly she nodded. The man had connections. Sourcing a luxury home like this for a short period was near impossible.

She waited. He had something to say, presumably details of how this arrangement would work. She watched him watching her and refused to ask. Instead she paced the big room, hands brushing custom-made cabinetry and slick stainless steel.

But eventually his silence was too much. 'About this arrangement, pretending to be partners—'

'Lovers.'

That baritone voice remained soft yet that single word made her pulse skitter. She paused, fingers clenching around the handle of the biggest fridge she'd ever seen.

She resumed walking towards the end of the room where sunlight streamed through French doors onto an impressive glass-and-wrought-iron table and cushion-covered chairs.

Rosamund turned to find his eyes on her. Even for a

woman used to public scrutiny, his intense regard made her almost self-conscious. 'As you say, a couple.'

When this man was involved she much preferred 'couple' to 'lovers'.

'So.' She focused on essentials. 'We'll be seen in public together. Are you coming to every event? I can give you the schedule.' Now she'd broken her silence she couldn't seem to stop.

'I have it and yes, wherever you go I'll be there.'

That should have reassured, considering what she'd heard about Ricardo and his nasty ways. Yet it sounded more like a challenge, even a threat, than a promise.

She was about to ask if he had appropriate clothes for the formal events but stopped the urge to babble. A man who conjured a multi-million-dollar luxury home in Paris could manage formal clothes.

She folded her arms, waiting for him to speak. Had he brought her here to discuss how to go about convincing people they were a couple?

Heat detonated low inside as she recalled her body's instantaneous, disturbing response to his.

To counter it she reminded herself they simply needed to be seen together. Public speculation and the voracious paparazzi would see to the rest.

They wouldn't attend events where public displays of affection were required. The most she'd have to do would be stand close and smile at him.

That could be a problem. She doubted if he knew how to smile back.

But Rosamund didn't really care if people believed the fiction. She refused even to note the stories the press ran about her and her apparent multitude of partners. Her lip curled and a tiny snort of disgust escaped.

His stare sharpened, his nostrils flaring as if in distaste. 'You have something to say? Something you want to get off your chest?'

As if she needed to explain herself to him!

'Nothing at all.' Suddenly fatigue swamped her. It had been a long day after a series of long days and the emotional strain of anticipating the next few days took its toll. She was both eager for this event and dreading it. 'Can you show me to my room?'

'Of course. I just thought you should know where the kitchen was. Security staff will monitor the premises but you won't see them. Otherwise there's no staff. You need to know where the food is so you can prepare your meals.'

Alone in this lovely house, free to keep her own hours when she wasn't attending an event? Despite the headache she'd fought since landing, Rosamund smiled. She could imagine herself breakfasting on the sun-drenched patio. 'Excellent. I'll enjoy that. Thank you.'

Rosamund surveyed the place she was to sleep for the next several nights. Tall-ceilinged and elegantly furnished, it managed to be welcoming despite the grandeur of both the sitting area and bedroom. A luxurious, modern bathroom was visible through an open door.

'It's a beautiful suite.'

She didn't care about the antiques or the grandeur. With pain now humming in her temples and growing by the minute, all she cared about was that bed. She imagined lying down and finally closing her eyes.

When she was alone.

She turned, and noticed another door. 'What's through there?'

She'd already turned the handle when Fotis Mavridis said, 'My room.'

Rosamund spun around, grateful for her hold on the doorknob when the world kept spinning and pain notched higher.

'You said I'd be here alone!'

He stood just inside her doorway, feet apart, hands folded across his broad chest, watching. She refused to admit it but she was beginning to find that too-steady gaze getting on her nerves.

Stupid when she'd spent her life under scrutiny. But this felt different.

You're tired, that's all.

'I said there'd be no staff. I'm your minder, remember?' His tone held a thread that might have been censure or sarcasm. It was hard to be sure over the painful thud of her pulse in her temples. 'I need to be close in case there's a threat.'

She looked down at the door then opened it and looked at the other side. 'There's no key.'

'If there's a problem I need to be able to get to you quickly.'

Oh, there's a problem all right. You're the problem.

As for him getting to her, he was already doing that.

No one since her father had got under her skin but this man excelled at it. Unlike her father, he even managed it with a few laconic phrases or raised eyebrow instead of a full-scale rant.

She turned to find him surveying her. His expression hadn't changed but abruptly she *felt* his self-satisfaction. He liked the fact this wasn't what she wanted.

Tomorrow she'd wonder why. For now she had other priorities.

Pushing weary shoulders back and drawing herself up

to her full height, she inclined her head. She'd learned to choose her battles.

Much as she hated the idea of him able to invade her privacy, it was obvious he had no intention of coming to her room. He might be smirking beneath that rigid stare, but he didn't want to get close to her any more than she wanted him to.

'How very sensible.' The pain now was so bad she didn't even attempt a smile. 'Now, if you'll excuse me, I'd like privacy.'

Without waiting for a reply she turned, picked up her bag and made for the bathroom.

By the time she'd taken some painkillers he was gone. She glanced at the connecting door and pursed her lips. Pulling out the chair at the writing desk near the window, she carried it across and propped it under the doorknob.

There was no key in the door to the hall and nothing she could use to bar it. She'd think about that later.

And about her compulsion to keep Fotis Mavridis at a distance. She didn't know why he unsettled her so much. It wasn't just his disapproval. She'd had years of that from her father. There was something else, gnawing at her, making her aware of him, making it impossible to ignore him.

Shucking her shoes and slipping off her jacket, she undid her hair with a sigh of relief and crawled onto the bed, letting herself relax fully as her body met the mattress. It seemed like forever since she'd been able to stop and switch off.

But her last thought was of eyes the colour of the sea, changeable and full of censure.

Fotis spent some time confirming arrangements with the security staff, checking the perimeter cameras and alarms and refamiliarising himself with her schedule.

So many days out of his own schedule to do this favour for the king of Cardona! But it would pay dividends in the end. Leon had promised his unwavering support for the initiative Fotis had finally got off the ground. *That* was all that mattered. For that he'd look after a bevy of beautiful, spoiled, narcissistic princesses!

As day turned to evening Fotis focused on his own work, checking in with staff, catching up on messages, and delving into a draft report on a particularly complex issue prepared by a new but promising staffer. It would need finessing before being presented to the client but the bones were good.

Rolling his shoulders, he realised he'd been sitting too long and glanced at the time.

He frowned. After making coffee and a sandwich hours ago, he'd retreated to his room. No matter his personal views on the woman on the other side of the door, he'd promised to protect her. It was unlikely any threat would reach her here, but he'd given his word. Fotis always kept his word.

Yet there'd been no sound from her room in hours. She hadn't gone to the kitchen for food or rung out for a delivery. Subconsciously he'd been listening for the sound of her moving around but there'd been nothing.

Why hadn't he realised before? He'd let the intriguing issues in his report distract him.

His mouth flattened as he acknowledged how determined he'd been to put her from his mind. Because thinking about her destroyed his concentration.

He'd let his response to her interfere with what had to be done. It was inexcusable.

Grimacing, Fotis moved to the connecting door and listened. Nothing. She had no light on but looking through the keyhole he saw something move. It took a heart-stopping second to realise it was a long, sheer curtain billowing at an open window, its movement caught by silvery moonlight.

She probably just liked fresh air. But the instinct that had kept him safe during his military career kicked in. He had to be sure. He turned the door handle, only to discover the door wouldn't budge.

Seconds later he was out of his room and in the corridor. Hand on her doorknob he paused, listening, but heard nothing. Silently he turned the knob, relief singing in his blood as the door opened without obstruction.

There was no sign of disturbance and he could see a form on the bed.

Keeping away from the light spilling through the windows, he moved soft-footed and silent along the wall, senses alert as he approached the bed.

It was definitely her. He recognised the pale trousers and dark camisole. He also recognised the sumptuous waves of reddish-blond hair loose around her shoulders, the arch of those definite eyebrows and the natural downturn at the corners of a mouth that in repose hinted at sultry sensuality.

His heart beat a quick tattoo as his lungs emptied then refilled.

Good to know she wasn't abducted on your watch, Mavridis.

The sarcastic voice sounded like his old special ops commander.

He dragged his attention from the way one breast looked about to slip free of her top. His hands flexed as he recalled her pebbled nipples hard against the silk as she gave him sass laced with contempt.

Not a woman he should hanker after.

Okay, she was here, but was she all right? Why was she

still dressed? She lay so still that she was either an incredibly deep sleeper or...

Fotis leaned over the bed until a drift of cinnamon and vanilla scent, laced with warm female, assaulted his nostrils. He drew it in, barely noticing his surprise that she should smell so sweetly wholesome. Wholesome but addictive.

Frowning, he moved closer and finally had the confirmation he needed. The softest waft of breath caressed his chin. He looked down and at last discerned the gentle rise and fall of her breasts which a moment before had seemed so still.

Abruptly he straightened and stepped back. She seemed safe enough. But she hadn't bothered to bathe or change, much less eat. What was her problem?

He hadn't wasted much time on a detailed background check. He'd already known more than enough about Princess Rosamund before her brother contacted him. He knew her character and her predilection for scandalous assignations. Was there also a drug habit? Was that why she hadn't changed or eaten and why she seemed so deeply asleep?

A quick sweep of the bathroom revealed nothing. But returning to her room he noticed something on her bedside table. Scooping it up and turning away, he inspected it with a penlight torch. Painkillers. Not heavy dose prescription medications but over-the-counter tablets in common use against headaches.

He switched off the torch and surveyed the sleeping woman, replaying their last encounter.

She'd looked pale, standing in the garage staring with wide eyes, and she'd blinked against the afternoon light coming into the kitchen. Then there was the way she'd hunched her shoulders, like someone in pain, though she'd been quick to straighten. The tiny lines puckering the centre of her forehead. He'd thought that due to temper. Could it have been pain?

It must have been bad for her to fall, fully clothed, onto the bed.

Fotis prided himself on his ability to notice things others didn't. To collect clues and transform them into a complete picture before other people had an inkling there was anything wrong. Hell, it was a core component of his business!

But he'd missed this. He'd let personal feelings hinder his ability to observe, collate facts and analyse.

No security system was inviolable. If there *had* been an intruder, Fotis might have been too late.

He put the tablets back and moved away so that light, sweet fragrance didn't tease him anymore.

His chest rose on a deep inhalation. Ignoring her wasn't good enough. He'd given his word to protect her. Despite his inclinations, he vowed that from now on he'd pay close attention to every move she made. He couldn't afford to miss any threat.

What had been a deeply annoying job had suddenly become almost impossible. He'd do it because he had no choice. But some primal self-knowledge was already screaming a warning.

He despised everything she stood for. Particularly her overweening sense of entitlement and selfish belief that she should get whatever and whoever she wanted with no thought to anyone else. But it wasn't just contempt he felt.

Brutal honesty forced him to admit to a thread, a powerful thread, of lust.

It had been there from the first and only strengthened each time she challenged him with those knowing grey-blue eyes and pert rejoinders. Her attitude as much as her body underpinned her sex appeal.

He'd thought, given his history, feeling such attraction would be impossible. Surely he had better taste.

Scowling, he stalked out of the room.

CHAPTER THREE

THE LIMOUSINE CRUISED down a street that housed some of Paris's most famous fashion showrooms. 'There's no need to come in,' she said. 'I'll text when I'm ready to leave.'

She didn't even look at him. Because she thought the person keeping her safe didn't deserve courtesy?

You weren't exactly courteous yesterday, were you? For once you didn't bother to hide your feelings.

Fotis ignored his double standard. He wasn't paid to be friendly. He wasn't even being paid!

Yet her curt dismissal rankled. He didn't want this woman's attention but he was stuck with her. He loathed people who took what they wanted without gratitude for those who made their lives easy.

But last night he'd promised himself not to take his eye off the ball. He couldn't let personal dislike interfere with that duty.

'I'll come in with you, no need to text.'

That earned him a sharp stare. Cool grey eyes surveyed him as if suspecting an ulterior motive. 'It's unnecessary.'

The car stopped and he glanced past her to the gold-and-cream awning leading into the showroom. The window display was artfully minimal and a couple of tourists took selfies.

'Don't worry, Princess. I won't follow you into the changing room.'

He watched her eyes widen fractionally and her mouth tighten. To his surprise he felt a tug of satisfaction in his belly, knowing he could pierce her complacency.

'Besides,' he murmured, 'it's the perfect chance to be seen together as a couple. It would be wise to give our fake relationship a trial in public before tonight's event. We need to look believable together.'

Her eyebrows lifted. 'Frankly I don't care if people believe we're a couple.'

'Do you really want to draw attention to the fact you need a bodyguard glued to your side rather than observing at a distance? That's guaranteed to attract public speculation. It would draw attention away from the event and fix it squarely on you.'

Maybe that was what she wanted.

But when she blinked he was surprised to read uncertainty in her expression.

Since they'd met she'd been supremely confident. For a bare second she looked almost vulnerable.

'Very well.' Her voice was clipped. 'You can come in. There's a lounge area where you can wait. As for our relationship...' Her head snapped around, eyes stormy. 'Don't say *anything*, even if asked.'

'Yes, ma'am,' he drawled. 'Whatever you say, ma'am.'

Did her lips twitch? He couldn't tell if it was amusement, annoyance, or a trick of the light. Before he could be sure she turned towards the door.

'Wait! Don't get out until I'm there.'

Did this woman have no idea of basic safety precautions? She *must* have had close personal protection before. It was an intrinsic part of being royal.

He filed that away to ponder later.

Fotis got out and walked around the rear of the limo. As arranged, the driver stayed behind the wheel, ready to accelerate to safety if need be. After surveying the street, Fotis opened the back door, keeping his focus more on their surroundings than her. A professional guard, a man he'd known in the military, strolled towards them down the pavement as if merely passing. Everything was under control as planned.

Yet Fotis' concentration splintered as he put his hand to her elbow to usher her towards the building.

The sudden, visceral response to his flesh touching hers stunned him. There was rocketing heat and a blast of awareness that made his fingers tighten on her cool, bare arm while everything inside him tensed. With *need*.

Forcing out the air trapped in his lungs, he withdrew his hand, holding it behind her back as they walked through the door that opened for them.

Repressing a scowl, Fotis nodded to the doorman and forced himself to take in their surroundings. The likelihood of a threat inside here was slim but even so…

Looking for threats took his mind off that powerful stab of awareness when he touched her. *Sexual awareness*.

Grim amusement eddied. It was laughable, of course. He wasn't masochistic enough to hanker after a woman like her. She had too much in common with his hedonistic, social butterfly mother, a type he'd always avoided. His reaction now was his body's way of reminding him he hadn't been with a desirable woman for…how long?

Fotis jerked his attention to his charge, now surrounded by fawning female attendants. He took his place beside her, preternaturally aware of her as if he'd entered a force field. His skin tingled and his hands flexed as a phantom drift of cinnamon teased his nostrils.

'This way please, Your Highness.' The older of the pair turned to him with a gracious smile. 'Monsieur.'

But her attention was clearly on her client as she led them to another room fitted with comfortable sofas, plush carpet and a raised podium surrounded by mirrors.

A third staff member arrived bearing a bottle of vintage champagne and a pair of tulip glasses.

The princess said, 'Thank you, but not for me.'

Fotis also declined a drink, and the offered canapés. He strolled the perimeter of the room, taking in the large, adjoining dressing room, entering just far enough to be sure there was no separate access to the space.

'No.' The single word sliced through the low murmur of voices like a blade through butter. 'Absolutely not.'

He swung around, senses on alert because, while his charge hadn't raised her voice, her implacable tone jarred. He stalked closer, curious.

'But, ma'am,' the older woman said, 'it's been arranged. The work has been done.'

'I'm sorry there's been confusion, but I intend to wear the dress I ordered last month. I wasn't consulted about a change.'

'Ah, in that case, let me show you.' The saleswoman's expression eased into a smile as she clicked her fingers and a minion hurried off. 'I'm sure, when you see it, you'll approve.'

The underling returned with a red dress draped over her arm. She cradled it as gently as a mother with a newborn child and the other attendants smiled enthusiastically.

'*Voilà!* With Your Highness's colouring and figure it will look spectacular.'

But Her Highness's expression wasn't enthusiastic. Fotis saw a ripple of emotion across her face, a frown on her brow and something stark in her eyes. A second later she smoothed her features. But there was tension in the set of her jaw and stiff shoulders. Anger?

Two attendants held the dress up between them. Even he could see it was stunning. On the right body it would stop traffic.

'As you see, that shade with your colouring—'

'No.' This time the princess's voice was the merest whisper, but it stopped the woman in mid flow. 'I won't wear it.'

'But Monsieur Gaudreau specifically requested it. It's been an honour to work on such an iconic piece. It will be the centrepiece of the whole...'

The princess turned her back on the mannequin and Fotis saw the other woman's smile disintegrate. 'I'll wear the dress I ordered. I assume it was completed?'

The other woman licked her lips, frowning. 'Of course, Your Highness. But this would mean so much, not just to Monsieur Gaudreau but to everyone who—'

'I'm sorry, madame. But it won't do.' She didn't sound sorry and Fotis saw the other attendants frown at each other, eyes wide with horror. 'I'll try on the dress I ordered.' When no one responded she added, 'Or I could wear an outfit I brought from Cardona.'

That caused a stir. Within seconds the red dress had disappeared, replaced by one in blue. The jubilant mood of minutes ago was replaced with awkward wariness.

Without glancing his way Princess Rosamund disappeared into the dressing room with several attendants.

What had just happened? Fotis was no expert on women's fashion. The red dress was stunning and it was clear from the reaction of the staff that her rejection of it was deeply shocking. He knew the significance of tonight's opening gala to the retrospective of Juliette Bernard's films. Especially for Antoine Gaudreau, an old man who'd worked with Bernard and was revered by many as something approaching a national icon.

Fotis' mouth twisted. Clearly her high and mightiness didn't take kindly to having their plans altered by anyone but her.

She'd reacted to the new dress as if they'd tried to foist a canvas sack on her, instead of a beautiful creation that would make her look a million dollars. Her refusal had to be sheer pique at having her plans thwarted. What other explanation could there be?

He'd known Princess Rosamund was selfish. Now he added callous to his list.

She'd ignored the staff's eagerness and the fact they'd clearly worked hard to produce the red dress. The fact it meant a lot to an old man at the very end of his career, and by the sound of it, many others, meant nothing to her.

She didn't care about others' feelings. Clearly she didn't subscribe to the idea that privilege came with responsibility to others.

Distaste soured his mouth and he reached for one of the canapés.

He'd been in her company less than twenty-four hours and couldn't wait to be rid of her.

Fotis spent the rest of the day in his own company. After the debacle at the couturier, and a stop at a famous store to buy a beribboned gift box of macarons, they'd returned to the house. He'd been with the princess only long enough to see her make a salad before she disappeared to eat in her room and spend the afternoon there.

He'd been startled by her easy competence in the kitchen,

whipping up a dressing and deftly chopping ingredients as if it were second nature.

What surprised him even more was that she'd left half the salad for him to save him getting his own lunch. Even now he found it hard to credit. She'd barely looked at him as she moved around the big kitchen, absorbed in her own thoughts.

Or determined to ignore the staff.

Yet the unexpected gesture was surprisingly generous. How did that fit with the spoiled persona?

Curious, he'd dug into the salad and found it surprisingly tasty.

There was that word again. *Surprising*. Fotis didn't like surprises. He preferred answers.

He'd spent much of the afternoon searching for more information on the woman he'd been blackmailed into minding. But there'd been nothing new, no startling revelations.

There were inevitable photos of her as a cute child, looking docile at grand events. A touching photo of her as a slender young girl at her mother's funeral. Then, when she was seventeen, a slew of behind-the-scenes snaps. Draped in the arms of a good-looking boy a few years older. Being helped out of a sports car, laughing in a barely-there dress, long legs on full display, wearing a smile that hinted at inebriation. Some that were more scandalous. Persistent stories of wild parties and decadent behaviour.

After that she'd been more circumspect. But always in the background were reports of her busy love life, her penchant for sophisticated parties and refusal to settle down. She had no job other than as a royal presence at various events and she lived off the royal purse.

Princess Rosamund seemed to have no aspirations to do anything to further herself.

She was another addicted to the privileges of wealth.

Memory conjured a woman with flashing dark eyes. His mother had a siren's ability to make you feel special. For as long as you had something she wanted. But behind the beauty was a corroded soul, interested only in her own pleasure.

With brutal efficiency Fotis shoved aside thoughts of his mother. He shrugged his shoulders into his dinner jacket and knocked on his charge's door. 'It's time.'

The sound of footsteps and the door opening startled him. He hadn't expected her to be punctual. Yet she was clearly ready, carrying a beaded purse and a transparent wrap of silver blue that matched her long dress.

He stepped back, giving her space, and himself time to acclimatise.

She was stunning.

Delectable, growled a husky inner voice. Not just husky but hungry. *Ravenous*.

Every male hormone hummed and Fotis registered a heavy awareness pooling in his groin.

Her reddish-blond hair was caught up with a few wisps artfully loose around her neck, drawing attention to its slim length and her bare shoulders. Miniscule straps held up a simple dress that skimmed her from breasts to toes. It wasn't tight, yet the way the light played across shimmering, shifting material revealed a body that made his mouth dry.

Want rose with a sharpness that left him short of air.

She turned to close the door and his gaze fastened on the smooth, golden flesh of her upper back.

Fotis felt the hard punch of response reverberate from his ribs to his belly, and lower.

He'd felt something similar last night, seeing her asleep. And before that, on the plane, when she'd looked so supercilious that he'd wanted to silence her sass with his mouth on hers.

Not. Going. To. Happen.

She was a client, even if an unwanted one.

He had too much self-respect to fall for the wiles of a woman so like his self-absorbed mother. *She* used men to get what she wanted. To her they were disposable. Even her innocent sons.

His voice grated over the bones of ancient hurt. 'We need to leave now if you want to arrive on time.'

Blue-grey eyes lifted and he caught Rosamund's curiosity. Unblinking, he met her stare, wishing she'd object to his brusqueness and break their deal in a fit of pique.

Disappointingly, she simply nodded and moved to the stairs.

Which meant he had to spend the evening at her side, smiling and pretending to enjoy himself. But not touching. Not even skimming his knuckle down her bare arm or testing the softness of those teasing strawberry-blond tendrils.

Fotis glowered as he accompanied her downstairs and into the waiting limousine. Bad enough to waste his time looking after a spoiled princess but to have his body quicken whenever she was around... It was the ultimate betrayal.

Fortunately keeping his mind on potential threats would give him no time to think about his sudden unaccountably bad taste in women.

Rosamund reminded herself she was used to discomfort. Royal duty was often tedious if not downright trying. But tonight she wished she could run away.

Impossible! She *wanted* to attend. This was important to her. She'd known it would be tough, but today's events at the couturier had thrown her more than she wanted to admit.

The idea of wearing that dress... It brought memories of the secret pain her mother had hidden behind optimism and a determination to look forward, not back. She wouldn't betray her mother's memory by wearing it.

She shuddered and bit her lip, turning to look at the passing view of Paris in the street lights, not wanting the man beside her to see—

'Are you cold? Do you want the air-conditioning changed?'

Silently she cursed his perspicacity. Fotis Mavridis saw too much. Whereas most men looked at her and saw what they wanted to see, she had the uncomfortable notion he was different.

Keeping her real self private had been the key to her survival. The thought of anyone breaching that barrier unnerved her. Usually she was confident about hiding her feelings and vulnerabilities. But today, anticipating tonight's event, she felt too raw, as if someone had scrubbed her skin with a steel brush until it bled.

Stop being a drama queen. You can do this! Think of all those years when your mother hid her feelings so successfully that the public had no inkling of her hurt.

But thinking of her mother only made everything worse. She'd been her rock. Rosamund missed her love, her guidance, her company. Sometimes she felt so terribly alone.

She dreaded tonight as much as she longed for it.

Rosamund sensed the big man beside her on the back seat shift his weight. 'Princess?'

'No, thank you. The temperature is fine.'

Schooling her features, she turned to look at him, but avoided his eyes. He'd make a stir tonight. Not handsome yet brutally attractive with severe features that had their own stark beauty. A superb body that looked just as good in a tuxedo as it did in a leather jacket and jeans.

What would he look like, naked?

She felt her eyes widen at the wayward thought and almost welcomed the distraction.

The press would have a field day when she arrived with him. It would fuel a whole new round of rumours and speculation. By tomorrow there'd be stories that she'd torn him away from his long-term love. Or that they were part of a scandalous love triangle. The options were endless.

After the press shredded her reputation, there'd been a stage when she'd frequented parties that veered towards the scandalous. No amount of effort had convinced her father or anyone else that she'd been an innocent, wronged by a vengeful lover. So in a fit of indignation she'd decided to live up to her party girl reputation.

That phase had been short. It wasn't the life she wanted. But though that was years ago, the press still typecast her as a shallow fun-seeker. No doubt tomorrow's stories about her and Mavridis would be salacious or full of innuendo.

At least Mavridis wouldn't look out of place at the formal event, or as her supposed lover.

Imagine the reaction if she'd turned up with the podgy, balding bureaucrat she'd first imagined him.

'Something amuses you?'

His low voice was a deep purr, brushing her skin and making her nipples bud. Instinctively she folded her arms across her body.

'I was just imagining how popular you'll be tonight. You could well have talent scouts approaching you. The place will be full of casting agents, among others.'

He didn't look impressed. She doubted much impressed this man. Certainly not her. 'I already have a job.'

'Just what does your business do, *Kyrie* Mavridis?'

'Fotis. We'll need to use first names in public.'

Silently, she formed the word in her head, wondering how it would taste on her tongue. Inexplicably she wished she could keep calling him by his surname. It felt safer.

'Of course. And your company?'

Unreadable eyes held hers. 'We provide confidential advice on complex matters to a range of clients.'

She raised her eyebrows. He made it sound like a state secret. Or did he think she was too dim-witted to understand whatever technicalities were involved?

Before she could ask anything else, the car halted and she became aware of the crowd thronging the pavement. At least he'd distracted her for a short time from the ordeal to come.

And, because of him, she wouldn't be walking into the gala with a full complement of security agents hemming her in and making her into even more of a spectacle.

Without thinking, she gave him a quick smile as he opened his door. 'Thank you for doing this for Leon.'

Minutes later they stood together on the red carpet, surrounded by camera flashes and demanding voices.

Her arm was through his, her hand resting on his forearm, the fine weave of his jacket soft beneath her fingertips. He was so solid, so steady that for the first time she wondered what it would be like to attend such events with a real partner. Not a stranger protecting her for commercial benefit, but someone who cared about *her*.

She thrust the idea aside and smiled for their audience.

It was an exclusive event, full of VIPs, but there were others here, hoping to catch a glimpse of the attendees. Many waved photos and some called her name.

They were about to climb the stairs into the imposing building when Rosamund halted. 'I'll be back soon.'

She moved to slip her arm free but he stopped her. 'Where you go, I go.'

It was a statement of fact. He was being paid to keep her safe, yet his words resonated powerfully.

She jerked her head up to meet that ocean-bright stare and felt a longing so powerful, so unexpected that for a second she forgot all about the crowd and the photographers.

Something had changed. It had started with that smile in the car. The one that transformed her face from haughty composure to something…genuine.

If you can believe that.

But despite his ingrained doubt, Fotis had seen a different woman in that smile. Someone impulsive and generous rather than arrogant and selfish. Princess Rosamund didn't want him around but it seemed she appreciated him for her brother's sake. As if the favour he did benefited the king rather than her. And she wanted her brother to be happy.

The shock of it had eddied through Fotis as he took his place at her door, standing between her and the crowd. He'd just regained his equilibrium when she'd slipped her arm through his, creating a quake of longing deep in his belly.

He'd been a paratrooper operating in difficult situations, then spent years carving out his business. Yet in that moment it felt as if nothing had tested his control as much as remaining aloof and alert while Rosamund of Cardona snuggled up to him.

Despite his hormonal rush, he could tell she wasn't trying to tease him. Her touch was light and impersonal.

A pity his body didn't think so. He'd never been so close to full, unwanted arousal in public since his teens. It should be impossible. But this woman turned everything upside down, even his instincts.

He made himself focus on the crowd, assessing body language, alert to sudden movements. But it was Rosamund's abrupt move that surprised him as she tried to slip away. 'I'll be back soon.'

His reaction was instantaneous, his grip tightening. 'Where you go, I go.'

She turned, bright eyes locking on his, and something behind his ribs tightened. Then she nodded and drew him towards the crowd on the side of the carpet away from the cameras.

It was only then that he realised some of the people calling her name weren't press, but members of the public. Instead of waving and making her way indoors, she approached with a smile on her face.

Instinct kicking in, he held her close and pulled her to a stop as he scanned the crowd. 'No. This isn't a good idea.'

She sent him a sideways look under her lashes that did ridiculous things to his hormones, especially when she leaned closer and he caught that delicious spice and warm woman scent that made him forget all the reasons she was poison. 'A few minutes. That's all.'

He was weaker than he'd thought, nodding even as he cursed his weakness.

He released her, keeping both hands free in case something went wrong. Anyone watching would guess he was hired muscle, but it didn't matter. He mightn't like her but he was damned if he'd let anyone get to her on his watch.

There were smiles all around and lots of excitement as she chatted with fans. She was good with the crowd. She made total strangers feel they were seen and appreciated.

But people-pleasing was a useful tool, not evidence of a good heart.

'If you want to get inside in time for the opening...' he murmured.

Finally she nodded and let herself be led away.

They followed the red carpet and he recognised several famous faces. They were about to enter the grand building when a man standing to one side caught his eye, but just as Fotis paused, senses alert, the stranger disappeared into the crowd.

Then they were inside the soaring space, resplendent with brilliant chandeliers and glittering guests. The crowd parted as they entered.

Training kicked in, making him focus on individuals, movements, anything out of place. When he heard the sharp hitch of his companion's breath, he was surprised, for he'd seen nothing to make him wary.

Her uptilted gaze was fixed on the far wall.

High up an image was projected. A stunning young woman with blue eyes and flame-red hair smiled as if the world were her playground. She wore red, a provocative dress that revealed lots of toned, honeyed flesh and clung lovingly to her sinuous body.

Of course he knew the photo. He suspected that image had featured in the wet dreams of men all around the world.

Juliette Bernard in the year she burst onto the cinema scene, causing a sensation. Tonight's opening party was an homage to a woman who'd won resounding critical acclaim for her craft.

Juliette Bernard, the English-French actress who'd later cemented her place in public mythology with her fairy-tale marriage to the King of Cardona.

He felt a quiver rack the woman beside him and turned to see her eyes, now more grey than blue and overbright.

Without allowing himself time to think, he stepped in front of her, blocking her from curious stares, and took both her hands. They were cold, but even as he registered that, she blinked and firmed her lips.

Fotis bent his head, surprised at his surge of concern. 'Are you all right?'

She blinked again and for a long moment emotion shimmered in that bright gaze. Grief so stark it sucked his breath away.

Then it disappeared. There was a flicker of a moment when something else softened her expression as she met his gaze. Gratitude? His hands involuntarily tightened.

But seconds later she was again the soignee socialite he'd met yesterday. A woman without a care and with the world at her feet.

'Your Highness.'

The princess looked past him and moved to greet the man who'd approached. She was gracious and charming, as if those moments of earthquaking emotion hadn't happened.

Fotis felt the world shift beneath his feet. It was unnerving to realise the woman he despised had hidden depths. That, despite her unforgivable actions in New York a month ago, she wasn't simply a shallow, selfish woman who trampled anyone to get what she wanted. That she *felt*, and felt deeply.

Who was the real Princess Rosamund?

And why did he want, badly, to uncover her secrets?

CHAPTER FOUR

Rosamund chewed her pencil, trying to concentrate. But her thoughts jumped all over the place.

Exhausted, she'd slept deeply last night and should feel refreshed. Instead she jangled with nervous energy. Partly it was from reliving last night's events and the emotional upheaval of being thrust into that star-strewn world about which her mother had been so ambivalent. The world which had been both fulfilling and destructive.

Yet it wasn't the evening spent as her mother's proxy that unsettled her. It was Fotis Mavridis.

She glanced across the patio to the open doors into the kitchen. He'd looked in again an hour ago, grabbed a drink and left, with barely a nod to acknowledge her presence.

His expression had been as dour as ever. No hint of a smile, not that she'd ever seen him smile. He'd looked as cold and blank, as judgemental, as ever.

Yet last night at the reception she could have sworn there'd been a change in him. When she'd held his arm heat had arced between them and despite his poker face she'd *felt* the spark of shared awareness.

More than that, he'd stunned her with that unexpected moment of understanding.

Despite all her preparation, Rosamund had been overwhelmed at the sight of her mother's image, while standing in the place where her mother should have been, accepting her accolades. For a second all she could think of was how much her mother had missed out on. And how much Rosamund still missed *her*.

The sight of Fotis blocking out the photo, and the crowd, leaning towards her with concern in his voice and sympathy in his eyes, had stunned her.

She'd known an all-consuming impulse to lean her head against his broad shoulder, breathe in his strength, and step off the merry-go-round of public expectation and royal duty.

For the tiniest instant it had felt like he *saw* her as no one else did. Saw deep inside to the turmoil, doubt and isolation. And understood.

There was something about that flash of solicitousness that told her he knew grief too. Knew the toll it took to keep pretending everything was okay.

Of course it wasn't true. Fotis Mavridis knew nothing about her, except, she guessed, the lurid headlines. He didn't know *her*, any more than she knew him. It had been wishful thinking. And, she admitted as she sipped her cold coffee, loneliness.

She put the cup down with a clunk and turned to the paragraph she was writing. She hadn't felt inspired all morning. But she was a professional and knew she couldn't wait for inspiration. Sometimes she had to coax it into appearing. Her editor, not to mention her readers, were waiting for the next book.

Frowning at the scrawl on the page she knew she'd be better spending her time doing something else. She slapped shut the notebook, secured the elastic band around it to stop any loose pages slipping out, and shoved back her chair.

She'd been here since dawn, trying to get ahead with her

story but all she had to show for it were ramblings she knew she couldn't use and a page full of doodles, cartoonish images of a severe-featured man whose eyes she couldn't capture. As if she could use *those* to illustrate the book!

Rosamund was at the coffee machine when a change in the atmosphere made her still. She looked towards the open French doors, expecting to see the daylight darkened by storm clouds, but it was still bright and sunny.

Yet the fine hairs at her nape and along her arms stood up. Slowly she turned.

Fotis Mavridis stood in the doorway, feet wide, arms folded, wearing faded jeans and an olive-green shirt with sleeves rolled up to reveal strong, sinewy forearms.

A weight plummeted from her chest to her abdomen, sending ripples of awareness radiating to every part of her body. Suddenly the peaceful room felt unnervingly different and out of kilter.

She lifted her gaze and met eyes that today glowed more green than blue. Heat fired her blood, warming her skin.

She turned back to the machine, grateful for something to do. 'Coffee?'

'I've had mine.'

His tone was brusque, telling her they were back to being enemies. That suited her. Disapproval and dislike she could deal with. That strange…yearning she'd felt around him was an aberration.

Her lips twisted as she frothed hot milk. 'Is there a car I can use, apart from the limousine?'

'Why?'

Rosamund bit her lip rather than blurt out an angry answer. For some reason he was trying to provoke her. She was tempted to wonder why he disliked her so much, but refused to waste mental effort on it. 'I have an appointment.'

When the silence extended she picked up her cup and turned. Only then did he say, 'There's no appointment in your diary until this evening.'

She refrained from rolling her eyes. 'I'm visiting a friend and I'd rather not take the limo. Is there a car I can use or shall I get a taxi?'

'I'll take you.'

'I'll be quite safe there. As I said, I'm visiting a friend.'

Yet her assurance only provoked a frown. 'How well do you know this *friend*?'

Rosamund blinked. If she didn't know better she'd think that sounded like pique or even... No, impossible to think it was jealousy.

'Well enough to know I'll be safe.' She refused to explain. She was entitled to privacy.

Strolling across the kitchen, she scooped up her notebook and stopped only because he blocked her exit. When he didn't move she sipped her coffee and let the familiar taste soothe her ruffled edges.

'If you'll excuse me, I'll get ready to leave.'

For a second she thought he'd refuse to move. Her pulse quickened and something like excitement jagged through her.

Finally he stepped aside with a mock bow, just far enough for her to exit. But he stood close enough for her to feel his body heat and detect the scent of soap and virile man.

Her nostrils quivered and that weight in her abdomen became a hollow ache as female hormones blasted into awareness.

Rosamund breathed out quickly, fighting the tug of attraction. It was horribly unfair that this provoking man aroused her. Silently she cursed her biological clock or whatever it was that made her susceptible.

He was waiting when she came downstairs carrying the enormous gift box of macarons.

'What's the address?'

Of course a greeting was too much to expect. But even surly, he commanded her attention. Damn the man!

She walked towards the garage. 'You can drive but you're not going in with me.'

'I don't care about your secrets, Princess. Whether your lover's married or why you want to keep your assignation quiet. I promised your brother I'd keep you safe and I intend to do just that. I need to check the place.'

Her lover!

Indignation rose, but it was quickly swamped by weariness. Her father had always judged her harshly, their characters too different for her to fit his expectations. The press had cast her into a convenient role years ago and now invented stories about her. It should be no surprise this stranger did the same.

Yet it infuriated her that he, like so many others, felt he had the right to jump to conclusions and condemn her.

Let him. She wouldn't waste her time on explanations.

As he took the box and secured it on the back seat of a gleaming grey four-wheel-drive, she slid into the front passenger seat and gave him the address, catching his frown at their destination.

'Well, well, well. Your macho man isn't such a prig after all.'

Rosamund looked up from the kitchen table where she was putting delicate, pastel-coloured macarons in a battered biscuit tin. 'Sorry?'

Lucie was peering outside. 'Your man, Fontis.'

'Fotis, and he's not my man.'

Which Lucie knew full well. The old lady's brain was

as sharp as ever. Rosamund caught her speculative glance and shook her head. 'Truly, Lucie. We barely speak and certainly don't like each other. It will be a relief to go our separate ways in a week.'

When they'd arrived, Fotis had insisted on coming to check out the flat. If he'd been surprised to meet a grey-haired woman in a wheelchair instead of a lover, he hadn't shown it. Rosamund had explained he was her temporary bodyguard—she had no intention of lying to her old friend—and shut the door on him as soon as he'd finished his security inspection.

But annoyingly, over the next two hours her thoughts kept straying to him. Was he standing guard outside the ground floor flat, or minding the luxury vehicle, since this area of social housing was known for its crime rate? She'd suggested he leave and return when she texted, but the set of his jaw and glitter in his eyes had told her what he thought of that.

'You take me for a fool, *cherie*?'

Rosamund looked up to see Lucie watching her, head tilted as if fascinated. 'Of course not. I'm telling you the truth. We can hardly stand to be in the same space as each other.'

'Get on each other's nerves, do you?'

Rosamund met Lucie's bright eyes and realisation dawned. 'You can't possibly think—'

'I don't *think*, I *know*. I may be old but there are some things you don't forget. The way you pretend not to look at each other, yet you're both completely attuned to each other. The air sizzled between you.' Lucie waved her hand as if fanning herself. 'And the intense stares when the other one isn't watching. Tss! I remember that heat.'

'Pure dislike,' Rosamund said quickly.

'You're not that naïve. And your mother would never raise a fool. There's more than dislike going on between you two.'

Rosamund caught her lip with her teeth. It wasn't true. Fotis had made his distaste obvious. He avoided her when he could. She'd never known anyone so eager to get away from her.

As for *her* feelings... Yes, there was a powerful physical attraction, but no one knew better than she not to trust that. Once, she'd naively let attraction lead her astray and years later she still paid for that mistake. She'd learnt her lesson. She found it hard to trust any man now.

'He tracks you with his eyes, did you know that?'

Rosamund's heart jerked hard against her ribs and she felt a betraying flutter low inside, but frowned and said, 'He's my bodyguard! He supposed to keep an eye on me.'

Lucie's voice softened. 'You're not as good an actor as your mother, *cherie*. But if you don't want to talk about it...'

She didn't. For some reason Fotis Mavridis loathed her. It was shaming to admit, even to herself, but she could neither fully reciprocate that feeling, nor conjure total disinterest.

'What are you looking at out there?'

She knew the view beyond the net curtain was of cracked concrete and overgrown wasteland.

'Come and see for yourself.'

Reluctantly, she crossed the small room to look through the opaque curtains.

Fotis wasn't waiting in an attitude of boredom or intent alertness. He was dribbling a basketball, weaving between a gang of teenagers before passing it to a huge youth with dreadlocks who shot it into a lopsided basketball hoop.

A ragged cheer went up and a smaller kid dashed in and grabbed the ball. Fotis cut a glance towards the flat then away, joining the ragtag group as it chased up the makeshift court.

Rosamund and Lucie watched for several minutes. The game was quick and the rules flexible and she was fascinated to see that while the locals gave no quarter, nor did they deliberately jostle the outsider. They accepted him.

Every couple of minutes he turned to look at the flat, clearly checking she didn't need him. Then he'd immerse himself in the game. Watching him move was a treat. He was agile and fast. She noticed he also shared the ball, including with the slower, less talented kids.

'You're right,' she murmured. 'Not such a prig after all.' Just with her. What had she done to warrant the judgemental attitude?

'Don't you have another event to prepare for?'

Rosamund dragged her attention from the action outside. 'Are you attending? I could collect you—'

'Not my scene. It never was. I was happy behind the cameras but not in the limelight. Now...' Lucie's suddenly stern voice brooked no opposition. 'It's time you left. I can see you haven't been sleeping. You'll need extra time with the concealer before tonight.'

Rosamund rolled her eyes, torn between a smile and chagrin that it was so obvious. But then Lucie was an expert. 'Yes, ma'am. Any other tips?'

'Only one.' The older woman reached up for a hug and squeezed tight. Rosamund returned it fervently. 'Stop tormenting yourself and sleep with the man. He mightn't be perfect, no man is, but I'd like to see you with a real sparkle in your eyes again.'

'You're very quiet.' His deep voice broke the silence.

Rosamund lifted one shoulder and watched the pedestrians strolling down the now tree-lined streets, so different from Lucie's neighbourhood. More than once she'd offered to help her find a new place but she'd refused, insisting the flat was home and she didn't want to leave.

'I could say the same to you.'

Tired of her circling thoughts, she turned to watch him drive. His dark hair was rumpled and there was a faint sheen to his olive skin, making her wonder if it would taste salty on the tongue.

Biting down a snatched sigh, she squeezed her thighs together, trying to ignore the thoughts Lucie's frank advice had unleashed. And the melting sensation between her legs.

For the last fifteen minutes she hadn't been able to eradicate thoughts of what it would be like to sleep with Fotis Mavridis.

Sleep! That's the last thing you want to do with him.

Lucie was right about one thing. Rosamund was attuned to him. He'd insisted on holding the car door open for her, which meant she'd passed close by him. The faintest tang of fresh male sweat and hot man lingered even now in her nostrils, teasing her. He smelled better than any cologne, better even than sunshine on mown grass or freshly baked bread.

She swallowed hard, again pushing away thoughts of licking his skin, tasting his mouth.

Maybe she should take Lucie's advice. But *not* with Fotis Mavridis. She wasn't masochistic enough to make herself vulnerable to a man who held her in contempt.

Though, now she thought about it, the look in his eyes as she'd moved past him into the four-wheel-drive hadn't been contempt. Nor had it been boredom. She'd felt the weight of his regard in every feminine corner of her body. Felt it again now as he cast her a sidelong look from narrowed eyes.

Heat shimmered in the air between them.

You're imagining things just because Lucie thought—

'Tell me about your friend. How do you know her?'

'Why? She's not a security threat.'

Did he grit his teeth? It would be some recompense to know she tested his patience as much he did hers.

'I'm just curious. You live in separate countries. You're a princess and she lives in social housing. How did you meet?'

'She was a friend of my mother's,' Rosamund said after a moment. It wasn't a secret, after all. 'She was a make-up artist and often worked with my mother. They did a lot of films together.'

'And you still keep in contact.'

Rosamund stared at his profile, trying to read his expression, but couldn't. She shrugged. 'She's a friend. I've known her all my life.'

She's the closest thing I have now to a mother.

Not that Lucie was particularly maternal, and she always brushed off Rosamund's offers of assistance, as she had Rosamund's mother's. But Lucie was genuine. She cared and was frank with her opinions and advice.

'She worked with your mother yet didn't attend the reception last night?'

'She doesn't have much patience for showbiz glitz and there were people there she didn't want to see.'

Lucie's outspokenness had won her many friends but powerful enemies too.

Seeing he was about to question her again, Rosamund asked one of her own. 'Why did you slip that kid your card?'

For a second deep-set eyes met hers from under winged black brows. 'You saw that?'

'Was it meant to be secret?'

'No.' But he lingered over the word as if wishing she hadn't noticed. Finally he said, 'I thought he had promise.'

'At basketball?'

To her astonishment the corner of his mouth quirked up, creating a tiny curling groove in his lean cheek. 'Hardly. But we got talking about maths. One of his friends was ribbing him about being a nerd.'

'Maths?'

That groove deepened and she stared, fascinated at what could almost be a hint of a shadow of a smile. Who'd have thought it of the iceman?

'You know, numbers. Algebra.'

'I do indeed.' She'd been a competent maths pupil but competent hadn't been enough for her father. He'd wanted excellence in all things. He'd engaged a university lecturer to give her extra tuition. How she'd hated those sessions.

'Why give him your card?'

'Because if I'm right about his promise, it would be a waste for him not to fulfil it. He's in his last year of school. I told him if he made it through the year with good marks, to contact me.'

Rosamund sat back in her seat, astounded. 'You offered him a job?'

'Of course not. I don't know enough about him. But, if he has the determination to finish, with decent grades, he could have potential.'

'To work for you? You need mathematicians?'

After a pause he nodded. 'It's one of the skill sets we use. But there's a big gap between raw talent and fulfilling it. I don't believe in holding out false promise. But if I'm right, we could find a university scholarship for him. If he grabs the opportunity and proves himself hard-working, it would help him build a career, even if not with my company.'

Flabbergasted, Rosamund stared as he focused on the

road, apparently unaware of how astonishing his actions were. She'd thought him many things but not philanthropic.

The fact it was a teenager he aimed to help impressed her too. That was the age, as she knew, when many fell through the cracks. 'You seemed to get on well with those teens.'

'You thought I wouldn't?'

She shrugged. 'People often respond well to cute children but can be less generous with older kids.'

'They all need support and encouragement, whatever their age. Too often kids are vulnerable.'

His tone made her instincts twitch. This mattered to him. 'Were you?'

He shot her a look designed to shut her down. Instead it heightened her suspicion that this was personal. His early days had been tough. 'Few of us have picture-perfect childhoods.'

A sharp laugh escaped before she could prevent it. 'You think *I* did? Don't believe everything you read.'

Her father had been a tartar, continually belittling his wife and daughter for being too friendly or informal. The vivacity and charisma he'd first admired in his wife had later enraged him, when he saw how small he looked in comparison. Rosamund took after her mother so had spent most of her life being berated and punished.

She looked away as they continued in silence.

But surreptitiously she watched his easy competence, driving through the congested streets. He had an alert confidence, an air of control, and she wondered what his story was. Her attempt to discover more about him online had revealed little.

He annoyed her and seemed to delight in showing how little he liked her. Yet she felt an uncanny certainty that he knew what he was doing, not just in protecting her, but in seeing promise in a Parisian schoolkid. He'd even won Lucie's approval, though she'd pretended not to be impressed.

But if his judgement were so good, why treat Rosamund as a pariah? She was on the verge of ignoring pride and asking when he said, 'You did an impressive job last night, playing to the cameras. Everyone bought your story.'

'Sorry?' She'd smiled and mingled but the edge to his voice told her he meant something else. 'What do you mean?'

'The photos of you gazing up at me with those big blue eyes. No one will question my presence at your side now. They won't think I'm a minder. They're all sure I'm your latest conquest.'

There it was again, the taint of scorn in his voice tightening around her like a whip, scoring her skin. Just as she'd begun to think he could act reasonably around her.

Silently she turned to stare at the busy street, surprised how much that hurt.

Much later, in the privacy of her room, she finally broke her self-imposed rule and searched for stories about last night's gala. Sure enough there were photos of her and Fotis Mavridis on the red carpet and more of them inside the splendid event.

For once the stories weren't focused solely on her. The reports were full of speculation about the 'reclusive businessman' who was rumoured to be a formidable force among international power brokers but rarely attended public events. Questions were posed about what they had in common and where they'd met. The avid conjecture meant public interest would only ramp up from here.

The vague hints about his power intrigued her but she, like the reporters, was distracted by the photo that got most coverage. It showed them looking into each other's eyes, him leaning so close that just seeing the image, she felt the phantom touch of his breath on her face.

Rosamund swallowed, discomfited. It looked like the most intimate of moments. His hands held hers and her face was upturned to his, eyes wide and lips parted. She looked like a woman yearning to be kissed. And he looked like a man about to claim his lover.

She dropped the phone as if burnt.

She remembered that moment, when the noise faded and the world eclipsed to a pair of sea-bright eyes and a man who, for a second, seemed to promise all she needed. But it had been an illusion.

Photos lied all the time. The child of an actor knew that better than most.

She'd been in shock last night, that was all. She'd expected there to be photos of her mother, but not that one and not so large. Though she should have known after Gaudreau's interference with the dress.

It had taken her a second to get a grip on her emotions, and she'd been thankful to him for giving her momentary respite from prying eyes.

But not, it seemed, from the cameras.

As for *his* expression, it was a trick of the light and the angle of the lens.

She snatched up the phone, stuffed it in her bag then left her room. Tonight surely wouldn't be as much of a trial as last night. After all, she'd spend much of it sitting in the dark watching a film.

At least if she felt emotional, she'd be safe from the cameras.

She was heading for the stairs when a voice drawled, 'So you *do* wear red.'

She swung around to see her minder emerging from his room. Again he looked spectacular in evening dress, his bespoke jacket moulding broad shoulders. The combination of silky black bow-tie and white shirt against his olive skin was lethally attractive. The midnight shadow across his jaw and the coiled energy she sensed in him made her think of a marauder, masquerading as a civilised man.

Rosamund ignored the jiggle of excitement deep inside. 'Is there some reason I shouldn't?'

The dress was one of her favourites, with a demure but flattering boat neckline that left the top of her shoulders bare and a full skirt that swished around her knees as she walked. It even had concealed pockets, though royal etiquette meant she wouldn't use them in public.

'After your temperamental performance at the couturier yesterday, I thought you had an aversion to the colour.'

Astonishment slammed into her and her bodice tightened as she fought for air. 'Temperamental performance?'

He sauntered towards her and she hated that even with that derisory expression he looked so good. That she noticed.

'A talented team of people worked hard to make it in a short period of time. Not just any dress but one that had great significance to the gala's guest of honour, Antoine Gaudreau. But none of that mattered to you, did it? You couldn't even unbend enough to accept a change to please other people.'

For a second she stood, stunned by his vitriol. Strangely—since she'd spent years telling herself the opinions of people who didn't know her couldn't affect her—she felt hurt. Until that was swamped by fury.

'You're misinformed, Kyrie Mavridis. Gaudreau directed several of my mother's films, including her first, but this week is a retrospective dedicated to *her* work, not his.' She paused and focused on keeping her voice steady, horrified to feel herself tremble at the sudden storm of emotions. 'As for the dress, you can keep your arrogant opinions to yourself. You have no idea of its significance.'

She turned and stalked down the stairs. It was too late to make other arrangements for tonight. But tomorrow she'd ditch her unwanted bodyguard, no matter what Leon said.

CHAPTER FIVE

SILENTLY FOTIS CURSED as the limo took them to tonight's event.

Princess Rosamund of Cardona didn't matter to him, except for the need to keep her safe. Her flawed character was none of his business. He should have left well enough alone.

But she had the unique knack of getting under his skin with her mixed messages, one minute haughty and selfish, the next apparently a considerate friend or happy to find time to chat with strangers for no apparent personal gain.

She'd hinted her past wasn't what it seemed.

In a bid for sympathy? Yet the starkness in that single huff of laughter had been real, he was sure of it.

She drove him crazy. And it wasn't just her mixed messages. For there was one message his body received loud and clear, and had from the moment he'd met her.

Attraction. Desire. Need.

Every time that visceral, unmistakable hunger raked its talons through his gut and clamped his groin, self-disgust stirred. Because that hunger made him a traitor to poor Dimi, who'd suffered because of this woman's casual cruelty. The princess hadn't cared about collateral damage when she'd decided to romp with someone else's man.

These feelings made him into a fool. Everything he knew

about himself, everything he'd learned about treacherous, selfish women, should have made it impossible for him to desire her. She shared the same remorseless selfishness as his mother.

Fotis had been a victim to that, but not the only one. He knew the damage she'd inflicted, still felt the trauma of it. Still carried the guilt of failing to save his brother.

His response to Rosamund of Cardona should be pure disgust, untrammelled by anything else.

And yet...

When she'd stepped out of her room in a dress that clasped her tight from breasts to narrow waist, that shimmered and rustled with every sashaying step...

He'd wanted her with a primal need that shattered logic. His body had surged in instant arousal. He'd seen the sheen of lustrous red-blond hair and all but felt its phantom slide against his greedy palms. He'd imagined anchoring his fists in it, tugging her head back to meet his mouth.

That was why he'd lashed out with that crack about the dress she'd refused. To remind himself, and her, that she wasn't worth his attention.

The ploy had backfired when she turned, her lush red lips an O of surprise. His imaginings had turned X-rated, his arousal threatening to become obvious at the idea of those lips on his naked body, pleasing him in all the ways he'd dreamed through the last two nights.

As well as surprise he'd seen a fleeting glimpse of hurt in her eyes that made him feel like a sadistic brute.

She was doing his head in and he was letting her, turning into someone he didn't like. Someone without the control he'd relied on all his life. Without that, what was he?

They approached tonight's venue. Another grand building, another red carpet, and lots more paparazzi, no doubt fed by last night's photos.

Fotis told himself it was her fault, looking up at him with those big, needy eyes, putting on a show for the crowd.

The difficulty was, he couldn't convince himself. He knew what he'd seen. She'd been genuinely distressed and he'd responded to her pain, wanting, despite everything, to ease it...

'Aren't we getting out?'

She didn't turn towards him, but then she'd ignored him the whole trip. Fotis knew an urgent desire to make her meet his eyes. He disliked the woman but having her ignore him was unbearable, though he deserved it.

'Wait,' he growled, pushing his door open.

He needed to get a grip, fast. Striding around the car he catalogued the crowd, thicker than last night and more excited, but nothing to raise an alert.

He opened the door and held his arm out to steady her. Last night she'd worn high heels but tonight she'd chosen spindly red stilettos. He didn't want to be catching her if she wrenched her ankle and fell on her face.

For a second she hesitated, looking at him under veiling lashes. Then she took his arm lightly, rising from the vehicle with an easy grace that sent his thoughts tumbling into the bedroom and the joys of a fit, limber lover.

As she stepped onto the pavement, an unexpected surge of movement from the crowd made him wrap his arm around her, jerking her close so abruptly she lost her balance and leaned against him.

'My purse,' she hissed under her breath.

Fotis bent to retrieve it. As he did so, a volley of voices called their names. Rising, he turned swiftly just as Rosamund turned in the opposite direction.

It would have been better if they'd knocked heads. Instead their noses met, and their mouths. It was so swift it took a moment for his brain to catch up. That was what he told himself later.

For now he simply responded instinctively, forgetting the crowd and his tumultuous emotions, tilting his head to one side and brushing his lips across hers. He felt her mouth tremble, felt the quiver run down her spine as he held her close. Then her lips parted under his and he tasted sweetness.

Bolts of lightning soldered his feet to the ground. He pulled her in, flush against him, drawing bewitching softness against a body turned to stone.

Her hand pressed to his chest, slipped under his jacket's lapel to settle over his thundering heart. He liked her touch, almost as much as he liked her delectable lips opening beneath his.

It took everything he had to drag himself free of the erotic fog clouding his brain. With a muffled groan that sounded disturbingly like surrender, he pulled back, straightening to his full height.

But the distance didn't obliterate his hunger. For a second longer her head was upturned, crimson lips parted and half-lidded eyes tempting him to kiss her, properly this time.

A wolf whistle pierced the hubbub and her eyes widened, body stiffening. She thrust against his chest as if to make him move. Of course she couldn't, but Fotis eased his hold around her waist and she took a step back. He felt her wobble but only for a second. When he knew she was steady he released her, hiding a grimace that felt like disappointment.

The noise of the crowd had become a roar. Cameras flashed as photographers fought for better positions.

Beneath the cacophony he heard a husky, cultured voice

swear in an undertone. Even her voice turned him on, making him wonder how she'd sound in the throes of ecstasy. How his name would sound if she cried it out in rapture.

Not helping, Mavridis.

His burgeoning erection would be visible soon if he couldn't stop it. Playing for time, he'd curved his lips into a smile, lowering his head so he could murmur in her ear. 'Any suggestions on how to play this, Princess?'

She shifted away, far enough that he could see her eyes blazed more blue than grey. 'We carry on as if nothing happened. Never excuse. Never explain.'

With those words she changed. It was like a cloak falling around her. He couldn't put his finger on it but she seemed taller, more aloof. She smiled directly up at him but there was no heat in her eyes, nor softness, nothing to indicate she'd quivered on the brink of capitulation just seconds ago.

She held out her hand and he placed her clutch purse in it. Then he held out his arm and she looped her other hand around it before they took their time going inside.

The evening was more of a trial than the previous night. Then he'd stood beside her as she charmed guests, scrupulously introducing him and including him in the conversation, though he played little part. He'd observed and kept watch as they moved through the throng.

Tonight was different. It was a screening of one of her mother's films. Which meant sitting beside her in the dark, close enough that he *felt* each move she made, heard too the occasional hitch of her breath.

It was Juliette Bernard's last film, made not long before she married and gave up acting. Instead of an ingenue or a sexy starlet, the woman on the screen was mature and riveting, eliciting emotion and engagement even from him. The story was poignant but ruthlessly realistic. No wonder both critics and the public raved about it.

What must it be like for her daughter, seeing her mother on the big screen, so long after she'd died? Beside him, his charge stirred. He glanced across and froze.

She wasn't aware of his scrutiny. She was utterly absorbed in the movie and in its shifting light he saw a solitary tear slide down her cheek.

His throat closed over useless words of sympathy. She wouldn't want him seeing her sadness.

But for the rest of the film, his focus wasn't on the movie. It was on the puzzle of Princess Rosamund.

He'd assumed she was a carbon copy of his mother, narcissistic and grasping. His mother had cared for no one but herself despite her ability to convince people to the contrary, at least for a while. He'd seen that again and again as she hunted for newer, richer husbands, ignoring her children except when it suited her to use them as decoys.

Rosamund on the other hand, was moved to tears, though her mother had died over a decade ago.

He reminded himself he wasn't here to analyse her, just stop Ricardo from hurting her. But Fotis felt disquiet, as if he'd made a fatal error. He hated uncertainty. His business was unravelling mysteries and protecting truth.

He needed to understand her. Maybe then she'd stop messing with his head.

It was late when they arrived at the house. Rosamund was weary yet wired. Too tired to sleep or work, too emotional.

'Fancy a drink?'

The click of her heels on parquetry faltered and she stopped, amazed. He wanted to share a drink? 'Why?'

They'd reached the bottom of the staircase that swept up

to the bedrooms. Wall sconces and a large pendant light lit the foyer, casting shadows across his steely features, somehow concealing more of his thoughts than they revealed.

'To clear the air.' His mouth firmed, eyebrows burrowing down into a V over that decisive nose. 'I need to apologise.'

It was the last thing she'd expected. Shock ran under her skin as she considered telling him what he could do with his apology. Tomorrow they'd go their separate ways. Whatever arrangement he had with Leon couldn't continue after his behaviour.

But she was intrigued.

By the fact he'd decided to apologise.

Plus there was the memory of that moment on the edge of the red carpet. She'd turned at the sound of her name just as he rose and turned his head, and their lips had met and clung. It could only have lasted seconds. But it had felt far longer.

She recalled the weighty beat of her pulse, her breathless anticipation. The faintest taste of him—unfamiliar and delicious. The hunger for more. And the look in his hooded eyes, a glow that turned her insides molten.

Facing public scrutiny after *that* would have been impossible if it hadn't been for a lifetime's training in appearing calm under stress.

'Okay.' She'd hear his apology, at least.

Soon she was ensconced in an armchair, sipping triple sec on ice while her nemesis sat opposite, frowning down at the fine brandy he swirled in his glass. The lights were low, casting shadows across his face that reminded her of her initial impression of him as a fallen angel. He looked powerful, brooding and starkly attractive.

His eyes met hers and energy crackled along her bones.

It was a mistake, spending time with him. She moved to put her glass on a side table when he spoke.

'I'm sorry. I was out of order, judging you over what happened at the couturier's. I shouldn't have spoken. It's not my business and you're right, I don't know the circumstances.'

Rosamund held his gaze then lifted her glass, letting the intense orange liqueur send a fiery trail from her tongue to her chilled middle. She welcomed the blast of heat.

'You made assumptions about me.'

Slowly he nodded. That frown and the almost sulky set of his sculpted mouth should repel, not entice.

Lucifer, whispered that voice in her head.

'I did.'

'Why?' She leaned forward. 'What made you think you have the right to judge me?'

It was something she'd wanted to ask so many times when people she didn't know criticised her unfairly. She'd believed she was reconciled to it as a necessary evil, given her family's position. But this time her accuser was here before her.

More, something about him had burrowed under her defences. His accusation had hurt.

'Because of what you did in New York.'

Her glass slammed onto the side table and she scooted to the edge of her seat, heart pounding so fast she felt nauseous.

It should be impossible. Leon would have double- and triple-checked this man but... 'You're a friend of Brad Ricardo?' Was he here to hurt her?

'No! I don't know the man, and I don't want to.'

The fingers she'd dug into the upholstered arms of the chair eased a little, yet she couldn't relax. 'If you're not a friend of his, then what's your problem?'

'The way you treated Dimi.'

'Dimi?' The man spoke in riddles.

If she thought him Lucifer-like earlier, the curling snarl of his lips made him positively demonic. 'Dimitria Politis. Or wasn't she important enough for you to remember her name?'

Understanding began to dawn. Rosamund sank back. 'You know her?'

'Yes, and I care when someone hurts her.'

For a split-second Rosamund felt envy for the young woman she'd met so briefly. She pushed it aside.

'So you *do* remember her,' he said softly. 'You just didn't care that you hurt her to get what you wanted.'

'You've got it wrong. I *saved* her.'

Now his knotted brow showed confusion rather than anger. 'That doesn't make sense. You'd never met before that night. She told me.'

Rosamund remembered the young Greek woman, gentle and a little timid but excited to be at the glamorous party. She'd liked her. And seen something in the twenty-one-year-old that reminded her of herself, long ago.

'No, I'd never seen her before, never heard of her. But...' How did she explain her sudden, emotional reaction to what she'd discovered that night? Her visceral response and her impulsive decision to deal with it. 'She was vulnerable. I wanted to protect her.'

Fotis regarded her with a stiletto-sharp scrutiny and definite disbelief. Rosamund held his stare.

Finally he said, 'You're implying you created a scandal to protect her? Why?' He leaned forward and she felt the air thicken. 'Why harm your reputation for a stranger?'

Rosamund reached for her glass and took a fortifying sip. It was tempting to explain. She *wanted* to clear the air. Wanted him to think well of her. Wasn't *that* worrying?

But in revealing her reasons, she'd have to skirt hurts and mistakes she'd put behind her years before.

'It's personal.' She paused, resisting the impulse to lick her suddenly dry lips. 'I'd need to know you wouldn't share what I have to say.'

'I don't betray confidences.'

If only it were that easy. 'I'd feel more inclined to trust you if I knew something about you.'

'What are you after?' His eyes narrowed. 'Commercial secrets?'

Despite the thrumming tension, Rosamund couldn't stifle her huff of laughter. 'Hardly. But you're an enigma. I don't know anything about you. Just that Leon believes you can protect me. And that you're judgemental, grumpy and rude.' And powerfully, shockingly male. 'I'm offering a quid pro quo. I'll tell you if you satisfy my curiosity.'

His expression was unreadable. 'What do you want to know?'

Even now he couldn't just agree. He had to probe and assess before committing himself. She recognised the tactic. She did it too.

In her case it was a self-protective habit she learned over time. Was he the same?

Fotis watched her eyes turn bleak. Was anything about this woman simple? He'd thought he had her measure when they met, but with every hour he had more questions and less certainty.

Maybe there was a scintilla of truth in her story. Maybe the photos in New York that caused a sensation meant nothing to a woman with her reputation. From her teens she'd been a wild child, teetering just on the right side of respectability but ever ready to party to excess. She lived off the royal purse yet her only repayment was attending a few official functions when she occasionally deigned to live in Cardona.

'How do you speak English so well? You sound like a native speaker, yet you're Greek. You live in Greece, don't you?'

Of all the things he'd imagined her asking, this wasn't one. 'I do. But I went to boarding school early. Most of my schooling was outside Greece.'

He waited, wondering what came next.

'Why did you agree to look after me when you have a business to run? What does my half-brother hold over you?'

Interesting that she didn't call him her brother. What was the story there?

Fotis swirled his brandy, inhaling its rich scent. 'He doesn't hold anything over me. But there's an initiative I want to see implemented. Something he supports too. He promised if I did this, he'd actively promote it at intergovernmental levels.'

He watched her think that over and decided to forestall her next obvious question by interrupting. She already regarded him as judgemental, grumpy and rude. Strange how that irked when it was completely deserved.

'Is that all?'

She shook her head. 'Tell me more about yourself.'

Fotis frowned. He had no intention of spilling private details.

But then her laugh, surprisingly rich and full, cleaved through his distrust to dance over his body, shimmering like summer heat just under his skin.

'If you could see your face! Don't worry, *Kyrie* Mavridis,' she said in that mocking tone he disliked but found himself increasingly enjoying. 'I'm not asking you to confess your dark secrets. Just let me in enough to know who I'm dealing with. What does your company do? How did you come to start it? That sort of thing. I want to know who you are so I can decide whether to trust you.'

That he could understand. 'I was in the military—'

'Doing what?'

'I was a paratrooper.'

'*That* explains why Leon thought you could keep me safe.' She leaned back. 'How did you go from that to running your own business?'

'I spent time in special operations and one aspect of that is intelligence. It was a good fit.'

At her enquiring look he continued. 'I was always good at maths. Once that's what I wanted to do, devote myself to pure mathematics.' Until Nico's death. 'I'm good with numbers, patterns, analysis and codes.'

'Ah. I begin to see the link.'

'The military was good to me but it didn't suit me longterm. I'd inherited some money and started a company providing cryptography and other services to government and industry. We protect information. We also analyse complex data and provide insights, sometimes about things other entities want kept secret. We provide a very specialised service.'

Her head tilted. 'Specialised and successful, since you don't have to advertise for work.' At his questioning stare she lifted one shoulder. 'I did an internet search and was surprised at how little I found.'

'There's no need for publicity, either for the company or myself. I prefer privacy.'

'Lucky you. I prefer privacy too but it's hard to come by.'

'Which brings us to New York and the scandal you created.'

She breathed out what sounded like a sigh. 'One last

question. Your company's services. They are available to anyone who pays?'

He held her gaze. 'Not to criminals, dictators or regimes that repress their people.'

'There'd be money to be made there.'

'We have our standards.'

'And so do I,' she said after the tiniest pause.

It was a direct challenge. She was taking him at his word. Would he do the same for her? Two days ago he wouldn't have believed anything she claimed. That had changed. 'Go on.'

She picked up her glass and took a slow sip.

'I'd never met your friend, or Ricardo. I saw them together at the party and was introduced but didn't spend much time with them. Later, I was on the roof terrace getting some air and overheard Ricardo and another man.'

Rosamund stared at the ornate marble fireplace. 'They thought they were alone. He was boasting about his little Greek innocent. How she was in love and he had her where he wanted her. She'd do anything for him.' Her lip curled. 'I'm paraphrasing. He was discussing money and sex and he was much cruder. He wanted her fortune. He didn't care about her.'

Fury streaked through Fotis. Ricardo was a lowlife, living beyond his means. Of course he was interested in a pretty innocent who also happened to be an heiress.

Fotis hadn't known about the romance then and would have put an end to it once he discovered what Ricardo was like. But given Dimi's fragile sense of self-worth and her history of depression, he'd have found a way to do it without breaking both her heart and her ego.

'Go on.'

Eyes that looked more silver than blue met his and Fotis

caught the hint of a flush on her cheekbones. 'He was pushing her to announce their engagement, but she wanted to tell her grandfather first. He was sure he could persuade her in the next day or so without the old man's knowledge. Once it was announced he knew she wouldn't back out.'

Fotis knew the old man, a friend of his dead father's, was unwell. It was one of the reasons he felt so protective of Dimi. His hands fisted on his thighs. 'Go on.'

Rosamund shrugged. 'I saw red. I'd only spoken to the girl for five minutes but she clearly had no idea what her lover was really like. *I* knew, so I acted.'

'You deliberately let yourself be caught in a compromising situation with him?' Fotis shook his head. 'You might be a princess but why would he give up an almost-fiancée for someone he'd never met? Marriage to an heiress would be better than a fling with you.'

A smile that wasn't a smile curved Rosamund's lips and her eyes glittered. 'Of course he didn't expect to marry me. But he likes sex and I *do* have a certain reputation.'

There'd been no particularly damning photos of her for years but her name was constantly linked with a passing parade of men, none of whom lasted long.

'I waited until the men were rejoining the party and accidentally bumped into him. I may have appeared a bit wobbly when I spilled my drink.' Her lips curled in a savage smile that made Fotis like her more. He had no doubt that despite the impression she'd given Ricardo, she'd been perfectly in control of her actions. 'He got me another drink and while he was gone I moved closer to the lights.

'When he returned we got better acquainted. It didn't take long. I knew people would be coming out to see the fireworks. All I had to do was make sure we were found in a clinch when they arrived with their phones.' Her voice held a razor-sharp edge. 'You know how people enjoy a scandal.'

Fotis remembered the photos. Her dress strap had hung down her arm and her gleaming hair was loose around her shoulders while Ricardo cupped her breast. He had her jammed up against a wall as they kissed and her bare leg was up near his hip. They were obviously moments away from sex.

Was her story true?

'Why not just tell Dimi?' The images had shattered her.

One shapely eyebrow arched. 'You think she'd have believed me, a stranger? Of course she wouldn't. She was besotted. She needed to see him for what he really was.'

'But why put yourself out for a stranger? You took the flak for those photos. Why not let her make her own mistakes?'

In his experience people rarely looked out for others, especially people they didn't know. In this case the gossip hadn't just been about the pair being caught in a compromising position, but about the princess being a man-eater, stealing a pretty innocent's partner from under her nose.

Rosamund's eyes met his and strong emotion arced between them. She wasn't amused now.

'I know what it's like to be in her position. I was even younger than her when I was seduced by a man who didn't care for me. I was just a means to an end. I wish I'd had someone to stand up for me then.'

CHAPTER SIX

THE NIGHT WAS BALMY, the company convivial and the vintage champagne excellent. There was even a huge, full moon hanging over the Mediterranean, creating a silvery path right up to where the sea lapped the shore below the spectacular villa. As if even nature were determined to add its lustre to the A-list event.

Rosamund had had a busy time in Paris and then in Cannes for the film festival, where there'd been a special screening of her mother's most famous film.

Tonight's party, along the coast from the festival, signalled the end. Tomorrow she'd go home.

And Fotis would return to Greece.

She sipped her champagne but suddenly it tasted stale.

She tried to focus on the conversation in the group surrounding her, and satisfaction that the events dedicated to her mother's memory had gone so well.

But her mind was elsewhere.

On the man standing proprietorially close beside her, so close she felt his body heat down her side. She should be used to it by now. They'd spent a week playing the role of lovers in public, attracting a huge amount of media attention. But after the night when she'd explained what happened in New York and they'd settled into a truce, the role had seemed insidiously more real.

It had become second nature to expect that ripple of awareness under her skin when he stood near. The tug in her belly when he bent his head, holding her gaze, as if unable to look away. And when he touched her, as he did so frequently now, the shimmering heat in her pelvis was utterly familiar.

It was all for show but her responses were real.

It was as if that night, when she'd shared what happened with Ricardo and Fotis had believed her, a vital part of her had been torn away. A part that had protected her from responding too much to any man.

There'd been men in her life since that catastrophe in her teens, but only a few. Nowhere near the number the voracious press implied. She'd learned to be discriminating and cautious.

What she felt now, with Fotis, wasn't cautious. It felt almost too big to hold inside. The thought of parting from him tomorrow created a poignant ache behind her ribs that was hard to bear.

It had become harder *not* to react to his touch, or more correctly not to reveal her reaction. Dislike had disintegrated. Now she discovered that had been her only effective barrier against his brand of brooding charisma.

She hadn't given him details of her experience, and he hadn't pressed, only reiterating his apology for judging her. But after that there'd been no disdain, no judgement. She often caught him looking at her in a totally new way. She couldn't read his thoughts but the weight of his gaze *felt* different.

She'd discovered a man unlike the frigid enemy she'd thought him.

He cared deeply for his friends and sought to protect them. He was reserved rather than overtly charming, but that reserve hid a quick mind and a thoughtfulness that surprised her, particularly when dealing with people who seemingly had little in common with a hugely successful entrepreneur.

She'd begun to understand just how successful. He might keep a low public profile but after a week in his presence she'd been impressed by the number of powerful men and women who wanted to spend time with him. Clearly his opinions and his company's services were valuable to governments and industry leaders.

A warm hand pressed against the small of her back, urging her forward as a waiter manoeuvred past with a tray. But when he'd passed, the large hand remained where it was, distracting her.

She shot Fotis a sideways look yet he didn't remove his hand. Gleaming eyes locked with hers and lightning speared her. She felt effervescence in her bloodstream and a tingle in suddenly heavy breasts that strained at the black velvet of her bodice.

Her breathing shallowed and she sucked air through parted lips, moving restlessly under his touch.

His attention dropped to her rising breasts in her low-cut bodice. Rosamund shifted her weight, aware of dampness blooming at the apex of her thighs.

All week this smouldering awareness had been brewing. All week she'd fought it, nervous of the neediness he inspired in her. Now that neediness blossomed into raw hunger.

He bent his head, murmuring in her ear. 'This is our last night in France. Do you want to spend the rest of it here?'

That velvet-over-gravel voice did appalling things to her self-control. Did he know?

But as he pulled back enough to meet her eyes she read his tension. It was in the broad frame of his shoulders and the tic of his pulse. His hand stroked a tiny circle low, low on her back and her buttocks tightened. She had to work not to flex her pelvis in response to that drugging touch.

You don't want an affair. You barely know him.

But how long since any man made you feel this way?

Rosamund sucked in more air, shoring up her resolve because *no* man had ever made her feel like this. Not even in her teens when she'd imagined herself head over heels in love with a suitor who turned out to be a scumbag.

Whatever this was, it was phenomenally powerful. *That* was what made it dangerous. Pursuing a relationship with him, however short, would be perilous to her peace of mind, no matter what her clamouring body said.

Did she really want a one-night stand with a man who'd awakened her in this way, knowing they'd separate tomorrow? He had business elsewhere and she was expected in Cardona, where hopefully she'd be safe until Ricardo was behind bars.

She stepped forward, forcing Fotis to drop his hand. It was the hardest thing she'd done in a long time. But it was for the best. Any entanglement with him threatened the placid, safe life she'd built.

'I'm afraid it's time we left,' she said to their host. 'It's an early start tomorrow.'

Through the murmurs of protest and regret she was supremely aware of Fotis, frowning, beside her.

When they left the group she caught Fotis' eye. 'If you want to stay at the party feel free. A driver can take me to the hotel. I need to pack. I have a busy schedule from tomorrow.'

She didn't explain that the schedule focused on her writing and she only had one royal engagement in the next few weeks. She could work almost anywhere. Including the Riviera, if she chose to accept the offer she'd heard in his voice and seen in those stunning eyes moments before.

'Where you go, I go, Princess.'

Once again those words affected her more than they should. She wondered what it would be like if they signified more than a bodyguard's determination to keep her safe.

Her neediness was only partly sexual. A week with Fotis Mavridis had scraped her bare of pretence, uncovering a powerful desire for affection. Partnership. Love. None of which she'd get from him.

That hadn't mattered in the past, because she'd learned to be pragmatic in her expectations of relationships. Yet, despite the almost overpowering need to lose herself in the pleasure they could share, she baulked.

Rosamund pressed her hand to her middle, trying to stop the useless yearning, then dropped it when he watched the movement as if fascinated.

'Thank you, Fotis. For everything.' She faced him, tilting her chin to hold his gaze, letting him hear finality in her voice. 'I appreciate everything you've done.'

She still marvelled that Leon had persuaded such a man to watch over her for a whole week. Whatever the favour he'd promised, it was obviously vital to her companion.

'No need for thanks.' He paused. 'You're sure, Rosamund?'

Anyone listening would have noted his gruff voice but only she understood what he didn't say. That if she said the word, they'd be lovers tonight.

Her throat constricted. It was ridiculous to want a man so much. Downright dangerous to want a man who, she sensed, might take a part of her with him when he left.

She nodded before she could change her mind as regret grew to an ache. 'Completely sure.'

He inclined his head then led her through the villa to the vast porte-cochère.

'Wait here while I get the car.'

Prestigious as the residence was, parking in the grounds was limited. Fotis had dropped her at the front door, then parked down the road.

'Couldn't we go together, just this once?' Having decided to be sensible, Rosamund found herself wanting to eke out her time with him, even just the few minutes it would take to walk to the vehicle. 'It's a beautiful night.'

She had the unnerving feeling he understood her internal battle. His scrutiny was thorough. Finally he said, 'Just this once,' in a voice so husky it abraded her senses and made her wish she dared change her mind.

He folded his hand around hers. They fitted together perfectly. Did he feel the tremor coursing through her?

'Come on, Princess. It's time we got you safely back.'

They followed a guard through the scented garden to a secret exit well away from the estate's grand entrance. The exit was around a curve in the road, out of sight of the coterie of waiting photographers. The guard paused, viewed the image of the street on his device, then unlocked the door.

Fotis paused, frowning. 'Actually, it's better that you wait in the grounds. I'll come back with the car.'

Rosamund shook her head. They had so little time left together. She didn't want to miss a moment. She'd decided to do the sensible, responsible thing and walk away from this man. Surely she deserved a few minutes more, walking beside him, feeling his hand on hers and the heat of his body close to hers.

'Please, Fotis.'

It was the first time she'd asked him for anything. Did he realise how out of character that was?

Gleaming eyes locked on hers and her breath caught. Finally he tugged her closer, and it felt…wonderful. Almost as wonderful as that moment in Paris when their lips had touched and she'd longed for it not to end.

'Come on, let's get you in the car.'

They passed several luxury vehicles parked up against the pavement, and were just about to pass a small van, when his stride changed. His hand tightened on hers as they slowed.

'What is it?' she whispered.

'The street light's out.' Belatedly she noticed the gloom. 'We'll go back to the villa and you can wait there.'

Rosamund was about to protest that there was enough light when there was a burst of movement ahead. A figure emerged from behind the van, lunging towards them.

Fotis shoved her behind him then leapt forward. She reeled, heart pounding. Between the shadows and his form blocking her view, she couldn't see what was happening. But it didn't sound pretty. There were grunts and a thud, then a loud crack that she told herself sickly couldn't be bone breaking.

Frantically she scanned the pavement for a weapon she could use to help Fotis.

A second later came the sound of splashing. There was a hiss of indrawn breath followed by a high-pitched shriek of pain that made all the fine hairs on her body stand on end.

The figures broke apart and she was relieved to see Fotis standing tall, broad shoulders heaving, whereas the other person—a man she saw now—writhed on the ground.

She started forward. 'Fotis—'

'Stay back!' His head whipped around to check she was okay. The other man wasn't. She heard incoherent sobbing from where he huddled on the ground against the van. 'Don't come closer but call an ambulance and the police.'

With shaking hands she pulled out her phone. She was aware of Fotis bending over the man and was happy to keep back. There was a strange smell in the air and that terrible, unnerving keening that sounded more animal than human.

The police must have been cruising the neighbourhood because soon cars appeared, washing the scene in lurid light.

People in uniforms crowded around, medics as well as police and over their heads Fotis watched her even as he spoke to them. She stood metres away, hands twisting together, heart still racing.

Someone had tried to attack them, attack her, and Fotis had saved her. Was he hurt? He didn't look it but she couldn't be sure. She started forward but he moved faster, murmuring something to the uniformed officer beside him then striding across to her. In the distance she saw other officers holding back a straggle of onlookers, some with phones raised.

'Come on, I'm taking you to the hotel. The police have agreed we can give a statement later.'

His jacket was gone, his shirt pale in the gloom as he put his arm around her shoulders and drew her against him. His warmth seeped into her and she burrowed close, so weak with relief that she trembled. Because he was okay. She kept reliving the moments of the struggle and her fear he'd be hurt.

A few vehicles away he bundled her into the car then took the driver's seat.

The interior light revealed his grim expression. She'd thought she'd seen him angry in the past but nothing before compared to this. Nostrils flared, mouth hard, the angle of his jaw screamed danger. He looked like some ancient god of war, indestructible and lethal.

But it wasn't his fury that stopped her breath. 'Don't shut the door!' She needed to see.

'What's wrong?' His gaze fixed on her.

Rosamund pointed at his shirtsleeve. The pristine white was marred by marks. Red marks. She stared, trying to make sense of what she saw. It took long seconds to realise they weren't stains smattered across the sleeve but holes. And through the holes, bloody flesh was visible.

'Fotis?' Her voice wasn't her own. 'What's that? You need to get it treated.'

He pulled the door closed and the light went off. 'Once I've seen you safely back to the room.'

He reached forward to start the ignition but she stopped him, her hand on his shoulder. 'Tell me what that is.' Her stomach churned, imagining the pain he must be in. The wounds were small but looked painfully raw.

'Tomorrow. I—'

'*Now*, or I march back there and get an answer from the police.'

A rough sigh broke the silence. When he spoke his voice was preternaturally calm. 'Some sort of acid. He had a canister of it.'

Bile rose in Rosamund's throat and she wondered if she might vomit. Her heart thundered in her ears and all her organs seemed to writhe in protest.

Someone, presumably sent by Brad Ricardo, had lain in wait for her with a canister of acid. Wanting to maim or maybe kill her.

Because of that Fotis was injured and undoubtedly in pain, despite his macho effort not to show it.

Her eyes squeezed shut. He was lucky he hadn't taken the full brunt of the acid. She assumed that in the melee it had spilled over their attacker.

'It's all right, Rosamund.' His voice was a rich, soothing velvet caress. 'Everything's okay.'

She shook her head, reeling. How could he think that? Why had she insisted on walking with him to the car? Because of her...

Her eyes snapped open to see him leaning in. She wanted to haul him close and not let him go. Instead she swallowed over the aching constriction in her throat and tried to find her voice.

'I'm sorry, Fotis. I wouldn't have had this happen to you for the world.'

'It's okay—'

'I can't thank you enough for protecting me.' She dragged in an unsteady breath. 'But don't patronise me.' She heard her voice wobble and sat straighter. 'It's not okay. Nothing like it. Now...' She reached to unbuckle her seat belt. 'We're going back. I'm not leaving until a medic checks you out.'

CHAPTER SEVEN

THE DAY DAWNED bright and clear, sunlight shimmering on the ocean from a sky of perfect cerulean blue. As if bad things couldn't happen here.

Fotis grimaced as he glanced at his bandaged arm with its low-grade hum of pain.

After his disturbed night, what he needed was a workout, a few hours in the gym or a swim to re-establish his equilibrium. But the medic had insisted he not get his injuries wet and though the exclusive coastal resort was well protected, Fotis refused to leave Rosamund alone in their separate suite, even to go to the hotel gym.

Being cooped up with her only increased his frustration. For the last ten minutes he'd watched her swim laps of their private pool, screened from the rest of the resort by high walls on two sides and a sheer drop to the sea on a third.

He'd spent the night reliving those moments when someone had tried to hurt her, but in his troubled dreams the man had succeeded. The screams he'd heard had been Rosamund's and it had jolted him awake, heart pounding and nausea bubbling.

But melded with his concern for her safety was something else. The fascination that had begun the moment he'd met her had morphed from disdain into rampant curiosity, through unwilling respect then admiration. And ever-present lust.

She wasn't the smug, selfish woman he'd imagined. He regularly saw her concern for others. Her wheelchair-bound friend in Paris. The people who gathered outside events just to catch a glimpse of her, and who'd been rewarded when she inevitably talked with them. Last night despite her shock at being targeted, it had been *him* she'd worried about.

Then there was the mind-boggling news that she'd acted to *help* Dimi, at huge cost to herself. That she herself had been a victim. Fotis had discovered a whole new level of feelings as he learned more about Rosamund. He was furious she'd put herself in danger, yet proud and protective. He wanted to find the man who'd hurt her and make him pay.

His hunger for her knew no bounds. Even last night when she turned him down, her actions had made him want her more.

For once her expression hadn't been guarded, so he'd witnessed the struggle, the decision to say no, because of course they had no future. They lived different lives. He'd seen what the refusal cost her. He too had felt that yearning for more as they walked in the soft darkness, hands clasped because that was the only touch they could permit.

He turned and reached for his phone.

Fifteen minutes later, Fotis stood at the end of the pool, watching her steady progress.

So much for the idea she expended her energy on partying. With her morning yoga, regular gym sessions and chamomile tea, she didn't fit the party girl mould. She liked champagne but didn't drink to excess. She'd relaxed and laughed, the sound of her husky amusement running through his body like fingertips on aroused flesh. But she'd turned down every offer to party except last night and they'd left that early.

She didn't fit *any* mould he knew. Whenever he thought he understood her, something happened to make him reassess.

She neared the end of the pool and he crouched, touching her outstretched arm. He felt a shiver ripple up her arm and pulled his hand away, rising to his full height.

She flicked bright hair off her face, her gaze making his blood quicken and the morning sun sharpen on his skin.

He gestured to the table positioned to make the most of the sea view. 'Breakfast.'

She hauled herself out, sunlight glistening on wet skin. On strong, supple legs. On her toned torso with that intriguing dip to her waist and flare of her hips. On the upper slopes of her heaving breasts.

Fotis' fingers tightened on the towel he held. He offered it to her and turned towards the breakfast he'd organised.

But as he crossed the terrace it wasn't the sea or the breakfast he saw but Rosamund. Her bikini was rainforest green, all lush foliage, with tiny dots of colour here and there. A red butterfly. A half-hidden blue Macaw. A pair of yellow eyes from a dark feline face. All designed to catch the eye, but none intrigued like the woman wearing it, her golden skin glowing with vitality.

His hands clenched and so did his lower body.

He sat and reached for the coffeepot. 'The police want us to stay longer.'

She settled opposite him, the towel wrapped around her body. He didn't know whether to be relieved or disappointed.

'For how long? We've told them everything we know. We're supposed to leave today.'

He read her tension. He knew the feeling. The sooner

they left the better. Staying with her in his Paris townhouse had been both surprisingly easy yet increasingly claustrophobic. Because he was aware of her in ways no bodyguard should be.

'You really want to pull the privilege card? What did you have in mind? Storming out of here as if the police don't have a job to do?'

He paused, knowing his anger was with himself, not her. Because he'd weakened last night and let her walk with him. Because he'd *wanted* her and that selfish decision had left her open to attack.

Because everything felt wrong this morning.

'Their investigation can only help you. If they can make a link between the man last night and Ricardo…'

'I know, I know.' She reached for her coffee but instead of drinking, held the mug in both hands as if needing its warmth. 'I'm overreacting. It's just that every time I think of last night—'

'You're safe, Rosamund.' He wanted to reach for her but forced his hands into immobility. 'Between me, the hotel security staff and the police…'

'I was thinking about *you*. You could have been badly injured.' Something in his chest pulled tight as her voice turned husky with fear for him. Her gaze dropped to his arm, making him wish he'd worn a long-sleeved shirt. 'How bad is the pain?'

'It's fine.' Though he was glad for the painkillers he'd taken. '*I'm* fine. We got off lightly.'

Unlike their attacker who was in critical care.

'Look at me, Rosamund.' When she did, that familiar spark of connection ignited again, worrying yet welcome. 'There's no point going over and over what happened last night and imagining a different outcome. We're both *fine*. You need to accept that, not fret about it.'

Her chin tilted and he welcomed that familiar hint of spirit. 'How do you know that's what I've been doing?'

Because I've been doing exactly that, imagining you hurt or worse.

'It's what people do after a traumatic event. But it won't help. It will just distress you more.'

She nodded. 'That's why I was swimming, trying to clear my head.' She gestured to his arm. 'You need to get it checked out properly today. We'll go to the hospital after breakfast.'

'Not the hospital.' It was unlikely Ricardo had another minion here ready to attack her, but Fotis wouldn't take that chance. 'I'll arrange a house call to the suite.'

'Why? What aren't you telling me?'

He repressed a sigh. 'The press got hold of the story. You saw how much attention we got in Paris.'

It had increased every day, with rampant speculation about their whirlwind romance. Their agreement not to comment on their relationship had only sent the press into a frenzy. The reclusive billionaire and the party-girl princess was too intriguing a proposition to ignore.

'There's a gang of photographers camped on the other side of the hotel. So unless you particularly want to run the gauntlet of the press, I vote we stay at the hotel until it's time to leave.'

He watched her face shutter. She'd never spoken of how press attention affected her and she always faced the cameras with apparent serenity. But a week at her side, often with his arm around her, meant he'd felt her muscles tighten each time they navigated the cameras. He had some idea what that show of calm cost her.

He respected her courage and determination not to let them see weakness.

'It doesn't bother you? What they're saying about us?'

He found himself hoping she hadn't read some of the more lurid headlines. Over the last week most reports had focused on the glamour of the events and of the photogenic royal, not to mention the fact she'd apparently enticed 'the world's most reclusive billionaire from his lair'. But others had twisted innocent situations with all sorts of negative speculation.

'Which bit do you mean?'

She gave a lopsided smile. 'I don't *read* them. I gave that up years ago.' Her voice was firm yet he discerned a note almost of vulnerability that made him feel something deep inside. Protectiveness? 'I mean generally, you and me being linked. It doesn't cause…complications for you?'

'Is this your way of asking if I'm in a relationship?'

'No! I just meant as a CEO, don't you have to be careful about your image?'

He regarded her closely, trying to read the truth behind those hazy blue eyes. Because he liked the idea she wanted him to be unattached? Because he wanted her to want him?

'I don't think being seen with a charming princess will harm my business. As for my image, I prefer to keep out of the limelight. But that's personal preference, not a necessity. Frankly, I don't pay attention to public speculation or what the media says about me.'

This week he'd made an exception. Since he'd agreed to undertake protection duties, his staff provided regular updates on media reports, as well as on Ricardo's whereabouts.

'I don't have a lover at the moment, if that's what you're worried about.' Something shifted in Rosamund's gaze. Interest? Relief? Was *that* why she'd turned him down last night? 'Do you?'

He hadn't intended to ask, but his tongue had a mind of its own.

Her shake of the head created a buzz of approval so strong it distracted him until she spoke again.

'What about your family? They don't take an interest in who you date?'

Dating seemed a curiously old-fashioned, almost innocent word. Fotis didn't date, he took women to bed. He didn't have emotional relationships with them. Not after watching his mother use sham affection for the males in her life, solely to get the lifestyle she craved. Besides, after losing his father and brother, he'd found it easier not to engage emotionally. His affairs were short-term, exclusive while they lasted, and with no expectation on either side that they'd lead to anything more than physical gratification.

'There's no one worrying about who I spend my time with.'

'No one? You don't have family?'

He hesitated on the brink of a terse response. Something sharp that would deter more questions. Except he knew now that Rosamund wasn't a spoilt socialite probing for fun. She'd been genuinely distressed and concerned for him last night, not leaving his side until he'd received treatment.

He couldn't remember the last time anyone had worried about him like that. It made him feel...raw. Yet part of him hankered for more.

His voice roughened. 'Only my mother and she doesn't take an interest in things like that.'

Blue eyes surveyed him, unblinking, making him wonder what was going on in Rosamund's quick brain. 'But if the press knows there was an incident last night—'

'She won't worry.' He saw Rosamund wasn't convinced. 'We're not in contact. I don't even know where she is. She could be incommunicado at some Pacific beach resort, or shopping in New York.'

It was a lie. Of course he knew where she was, on a luxurious, privately-owned Caribbean island. Even after all these years he kept discreet tabs on the woman. If he knew where she was he could ensure their paths never crossed.

Time to change the subject.

'I talked with your brother.'

'Leon? He rang?' Fotis heard pleased surprise in her voice. As if a call from the king was an unexpected pleasure. What were *her* family relationships like? He doubted they could be worse than his.

'I called to update him.' He paused. 'The US investigators are closing in on Ricardo. They're hopeful it won't take much longer to finish building the case and arrest him. But you'll need continued close personal protection for a while longer.'

If he'd expected her to be pleased, he was mistaken.

'He's already tried an attack on me and failed. The police have the attacker in custody.'

'They've yet to prove the link and that doesn't mean you're out of danger. What's to stop Ricardo trying again?'

Rosamund paled. 'Is that likely? Surely he has other priorities if he's running out of money.'

Fotis' mouth flattened. He knew how reckless a thwarted narcissist could be, his mother was a perfect example. Ricardo might not expect money from Rosamund, but Fotis guessed he felt she owed him for what he'd lost.

He leaned across the table, willing her to understand. 'You made a fool of him in public. You denied him the fortune he desperately needed. And he *is* desperate. That makes him angry and dangerous. The scandal you created means even if he did have another woman in his sights, they wouldn't trust him after reading those press reports. If he's going down, he'll want to take you with him.'

Fotis saw the brutal words sink in, hating their necessity.

Rosamund gave a shuddering sigh then put her untouched coffee down. 'So Leon wants me to have the full complement of royal bodyguards when I get back to Cardona.'

'That's one option.' Fotis measured his words carefully. 'Or you could come with me to Greece. I can protect you there more easily. After all, the world believes we're lovers.' He ignored the blast of pleasure his words elicited. 'No one will think it suspicious if we spend time together.'

'To Greece? With you?'

Her astonishment was such that he might have suggested they fly to the moon instead of across the Mediterranean.

'You don't trust me to look after you?'

Her gaze went to his bandaged arm then to his face. 'Of course I trust you.'

There it was again, that peculiar feeling of loosening and warmth, deep inside, as if she'd tugged free a too-tight knot in his gut. He didn't let himself wonder why her trust mattered.

'Why would you do that? You fulfilled your end of the bargain. Leon will deliver on his promise.'

Fotis was the first to look away, fixing his attention on the navy blue sea. 'There are benefits to having a king in your debt.'

'You negotiated another deal with him?'

He shrugged. Let her think that. It was easier to let her believe his interest was in fulfilling his own agenda than a simple determination to keep her safe.

He cared about her well-being.

That was rare. For years he'd cut himself off from relationships. There were few exceptions, like Dimi Politis and her grandfather. Life was easier when you were totally self-sufficient. And far less painful.

'He should have spoken to me before making any arrangements.'

She folded her arms, inadvertently tugging the towel down to reveal her breasts, plumped up by the gesture. Fotis made himself look away, wrestling his unruly thoughts under control. He couldn't be distracted by that lush body and what he'd like to do with her.

'I have a busy schedule. I can't just hare off to Greece.'

'Leon had someone check your royal diary. He said there's nothing that can't be rescheduled.'

The look she gave him ignited, as if he'd poured petrol onto hot embers. Her eyes blazed and perversely he wanted to draw closer and bask in that heat.

'I haven't been living in Cardona full-time lately. Leon has no idea of my schedule.' She bit the words out, all clipped indignation. 'Not all my commitments are in the royal diary.'

Fotis crossed his arms. 'Is there somewhere else you need to be in the next week or so? Something else you need to do?'

A suspicion had formed over their time in Paris. They'd attended a lot of events together. Some expected, like formal galas and film screenings. Some surprising, like a community college awards night where Rosamund had presented scholarships to teenagers studying acting and related disciplines. Scholarships in her mother's name.

Rosamund wasn't the woman he'd first imagined. But as time passed he'd seen the hours she'd spent frowning over her laptop, or engrossed, writing in a tattered notebook. Both of which she'd snap shut whenever he approached.

He supposed he could confirm his suspicion easily enough, but he didn't want to investigate her any more than he already had. She'd had enough people pry into her life.

He'd rather she told him herself.

'Rosamund?'

She firmed her lips and looked away. Her schedule for the next month consisted of solid days working on the draft of her new book, and ideas for illustrations. But she was *not* going to explain that. The idea of spending more time with him made her feel vulnerable. She'd had enough trouble trying to get work done this last week, always hyper-alert to his presence in the Paris house.

Her life wasn't perfect but it suited her. She was heart whole and set her own priorities. That had always been enough for her, hadn't it?

Yet having him at her side, looking out for her, had made her wonder what it would be like to be with someone. *Really* be with someone. To *matter to them*.

As if you'd ever matter to Fotis. He's only here because he's done a deal with Leon.

Rosamund remembered his contempt when they'd met. She understood his anger at what he thought she'd done to Dimitria Politis. After a lifetime of being judged and found wanting, Rosamund resented that he'd done exactly that.

She deserved better. Far better.

And maybe you're scrounging for reasons to keep your distance. When you explained what happened in New York, he believed you. He stopped being so judgemental.

Maybe you're jealous of the Greek girl who arouses him

to such protectiveness. Last night it was all you could do to resist tumbling into his bed.

Her problem was that this man made her feel unfamiliar emotions. As if it weren't enough that she was targeted by an unbalanced criminal.

Her mouth tugged down in a rueful half-smile. Life was never simple, was it?

'I don't like people talking about me behind my back.' Which was hilarious, when she thought about it. That was the story of her life. 'Organising things on my behalf, I mean.'

She'd hoped, after that recent meeting with Leon, that perhaps she was more to her half-brother than an unwanted responsibility. It was stupid to feel hurt that he'd discussed the situation with Fotis, not her. After all, Fotis had called him. Rosamund had been too shell-shocked last night to call Leon. For most of her early years he hadn't been around. She'd certainly never got in the habit of confiding in him.

She was simply out of sorts today. She didn't know what she wanted. That exasperated her. She never dithered.

Rosamund turned to meet Fotis' intense stare. It felt like diving into the ocean, letting the currents drag her deep. As if she could float there safely.

The intensity of the illusion pushed her into speech. 'I don't want a bodyguard, even for another week.'

She didn't want to feel beholden, knowing he saw her as an obligation. The physical pull between them might be strong but one glance at that proud face reminded her Fotis' priorities would always be business.

'But,' she said as he opened his mouth, 'I'll consider going with you to Greece.'

No! This is a mistake.

She silenced the warning voice in her head. Just as she

ignored her illicit thrill at the idea of going to Greece with him. Last night she'd told herself parting from him was necessary. Today her willpower had seriously fractured. The thought of leaving him filled her with dread.

Those winged, black eyebrows lifted. 'You'll consider it?'

'On one condition. First, we go to the hospital and get your arm checked properly, not by the house doctor here, but by an expert. Then—'

'That's two conditions.'

'Live with it, Fotis. This is non-negotiable.' She waited until he inclined his head. 'Secondly, we lunch today at a venue of my choice. Not here in the hotel but somewhere public.'

He frowned. 'Didn't you hear what I said about possible danger?'

'I heard it and I have no intention of putting either of us at risk. At the same time, I hate that Brad Ricardo is affecting what I can and can't do. That he's hurt you—'

'I'll recover. As for what you can do, it's not for much longer. The police will find the connection between last night's attacker and Ricardo. He'll pay, I promise you.'

Warmth spread as his words sank deep. She heard his sincerity, read it in the determined angle of his jaw and the promise in his eyes.

'I believe you. But this isn't just about Ricardo. It's about having my actions dictated by others. I refuse to let that man, or the press, force me to cower in a hotel suite, no matter how luxurious. I want to show them, and myself, that I make my own choices. I'm not running scared.'

It was how she operated. In her teens she'd struggled to cope with the outpouring of negativity from her father and the press. The stories they'd printed, most pure fiction, had made her cringe and retreat into herself.

Until she realised she was building a prison for herself. That was when she'd decided to live up to her father's expectations, for a few months seeking out scandalous parties just to annoy him. But it wasn't what she wanted, just bravado in the face of deep hurt and loneliness.

That was a long time ago. Since then she'd carved her own life, undertaking royal duties but mainly concentrating on her own work. It was a matter of pride to put on a public face and ignore the negative comments, especially when she attended high-profile events. She mightn't read the gossip but she heard enough to know she was still fair game for the press. She wouldn't, *couldn't* stop now. Because hiding equated to weakness and she'd vowed always to be strong when it came to the press.

She drew a deep breath. 'Those are my conditions. A hospital check, a session with the police, then lunch out.'

From his grim expression she expected an argument, if not downright refusal. So it felt ridiculously like a victory when he inclined his head.

Several hours later they were seated at the premier table in the Riviera's most exclusive restaurant. Of course they'd had no trouble getting a table. Set apart from the other diners, they were on an expansive terrace with a phenomenal view of the Côte d'Azur. Below the terrace an unscalable wall dropped to the road below. They were safe from intruders.

A crowd of photographers had followed them from their hotel to the hospital, then a growing number from the hospital to the restaurant. Plain-clothed security guards had held the crowd back as she and Fotis entered the building.

Rosamund had kept her chin up as she stepped from the car, confident in a stunning blue dress that brought out the colour in her eyes.

It was only when Fotis leaned close and whispered, 'Don't look so fierce,' that she'd remembered to smile.

After that, it was easy to play her part, for he'd looped his arm around her hip and drawn her close. It had been the most natural thing in the world to snuggle up to him, the shouts of photographers blurring into white noise.

Now he sat relaxed, watching her over the remains of his dessert. He was resplendent in a tailored jacket and trousers with an open shirt of pale aquamarine that made his skin look like bronze, his eyes like the sea.

'Was it worth it? Coming here?'

She shrugged. Perhaps it seemed petty to him, her need to show herself uncowed. But the attack on him last night had left her feeling close to undone. Today's outing might be symbolic but it was important to her. In her experience, appearing strong was the first step to being strong.

'Absolutely. Not just because of the press. I've enjoyed our meal. Thanks for coming with me.'

The food had been superb but the company had made it special. It was the first time they'd shared a meal and it had been remarkably easy. The conversation had been engaging, never awkward, and she felt more relaxed than she had in days. In fact, the meal she'd planned as a defiant gesture had turned into a delight.

'My pleasure.' His half-smile warmed her as they left the table, detouring across the terrace and pausing to admire the view. 'So, Greece?'

Rosamund turned to find him a breath away. Her pulse galloped.

He didn't look like a man who saw her as a responsibility. The hot glint in his eyes didn't signal detached professionalism. It matched the hunger that roared through her blood, a suddenly unstoppable force.

She'd spent her life learning *not* to be impulsive, overcoming her natural spontaneity and thinking before she acted. But he was so close, and she'd resisted so long.

And she'd been so worried about him since last night.

Suddenly she couldn't find the willpower to hold back any longer.

She lifted her hand, feeling the scrape of his close-shaved beard, the heat of his flesh and the strength of his powerful jaw. Her breath hitched as pleasure spread from her sensitive palm. Her nipples budded against her dress, more sensitive without a bra, and her breath escaped on a rush of reckless excitement.

Rosamund raised her head and brushed her lips against his, and the world disappeared.

CHAPTER EIGHT

THERE IT WAS, the jolt of connection, the instant hunger. Heat and fire and a whole maelstrom of feelings rushing inside him as her mouth touched his.

He'd seen the kiss coming. He'd had plenty of time to stop it and hadn't. It was like last time, when an accidental meeting of mouths had undone him.

This time he'd had a choice. But how could there be a choice when his craving for her grew so great it kept him from sleep? From concentrating on work, from everything but thoughts of her?

Fotis looped his arms around her, hauling her in, slicking the open seam of her lips and pushing in to taste her.

She tasted like chocolate, courtesy of the handmade truffle she'd had instead of dessert. And of warm, luscious woman. He angled his head, delving deep, drawing her closer, repressing a sigh of satisfaction at the feel of her breasts crushed against his body and her hands slipping around his neck, pulling his head down to hers.

She smelt of cinnamon, vanilla and needy female.

Her low hum of pleasure tickled his tongue. It pulled his skin tight and weighted his hands as they slid around to grasp her hips and hold her close.

He drew her tongue into his mouth, sucking hard as blood pooled in his groin. He wanted...

Sounds intruded. For a second he couldn't even identify it as a sound, just in awareness of something else, something beyond the pair of them. Then, finally he heard a voice calling their names.

The world crashed back. Even then, knowing they weren't alone, it took everything he had to lift his mouth from hers. And more again to withstand temptation when he saw her, eyes closed and lips parted, rising on her toes to follow his retreat as if she *needed* his kisses.

Another shout destroyed the illusion of intimacy.

From the corner of his eye he saw, on the road below them, a photographer with a massive telephoto lens trained on them. Instinctively, Fotis swung around, shielding Rosamund from view.

Was that why she'd wandered over here? To give the press fodder for their stories?

At least they were screened from the other diners in the restaurant by a collection of large, potted oleanders.

His fingers tightened on her hips. Had she used him to make her point that she was unfazed by last night's threat? To feed the story they were lovers? His lips twisted as a sour tang filled his mouth. But then she opened her eyes, looking dazed and undone. Unguarded. And the beginnings of anger clenching his belly dissipated.

Anyway, what did any photos matter? He didn't care what the press printed about him. A photo of them kissing was hardly a disaster. It only rankled momentarily because of his inveterate disgust at being used.

But looking down into those slumbrous eyes, he couldn't believe she was anything like the woman who'd used him as a convenient puppet time and again. Rosamund was complex and not easy to read but she wasn't like his mother who'd brought out her sons only when she needed them, then shunted them off and forgotten them as soon as she had what she wanted.

He remembered Rosamund in Paris with those eager teens. Her interest in them had been genuine. She'd stayed late at the awards ceremony, alight with enthusiasm as they talked about their aspirations.

'Fotis?'

'Did you know about the photographer?'

Rosamund frowned. 'Photographer?' She swung around towards the restaurant, dislodging his hold, and he had his answer. She looked baffled as she surveyed the thick foliage between them and the other diners. 'They'll be at the entrance, waiting for us to come out. Is that what you mean?'

He shook his head. 'It doesn't matter.'

It was a lie. It *did* matter. Not the photographer, but Fotis' reaction to that kiss. The mere touch of her lips and he'd dropped all pretence of staying alert to protect her from danger. What had happened to his laser-sharp focus? The instincts he'd always relied on? His need for caution while responsible for her safety?

The barrier separating him from others that had become innate over the years.

A frisson of warning skimmed his spine. Even with lovers, sharing the most intimate passion, Fotis never gave up his whole self. Yet with Rosamund a simple kiss made him lose himself.

He forced himself into speech. 'There's a photographer down on the road. He must have grown tired of waiting for us to leave.'

Rosamund's face flushed and her mouth set in a straight line. But her lips were still full from their kiss and he knew a crazy urge to forget where they were and resume what they'd just started.

'He saw us?'

'Saw and photographed. But it doesn't matter. You wanted to prove to Ricardo you're not hiding in a corner. We definitely succeeded.'

She frowned and looked like she was about to protest.

'It's done, Rosamund. No point fretting about it.'

After a second or two she nodded and his admiration grew. He had some inkling how hard she found the intrusive press attention. He'd only been subjected to it occasionally but she'd faced it all her life. Instead of ranting about it she moved on, choosing to put it aside.

That took courage. And incredible determination.

As he watched, her posture and expression changed, tiny alterations he could barely catalogue. But within moments she transformed from the unguarded, sensual woman he'd just kissed into a princess, serene and aloof. He felt a pang of loss.

Yet her lips were plumper than before and her eyes held a hazy shimmer that, this close, spoke of arousal.

Heat shafted through his lower body and his hands flexed against the need to reach out and ruffle her newfound poise. To pull her hard against him and make them both forget photographs and headlines and duty.

But he had to keep her safe. Not ravish her in public. So he took her arm and they walked through the restaurant, nodding to a couple of acquaintances and thanking the staff.

No one else knew he still tasted her on his tongue. That her sweet and spice scent teased his nostrils. That his body was tense with the memory of her lithe waist in his hands and the delicious curve of her body, straining against him.

His task was a thousand times more difficult than before. How could he ignore the way she made him feel, so he could keep her safe?

The sun was low as they flew across a scattering of islands so tiny they looked like pearls against the deep blue sea.

Now they reached a larger island and the helicopter began to descend. The land rose steeply from the shoreline to a razorback ridge topped by a row of ruined windmills. They were roofless stone shells. Only the last one was whole, whitewashed and with sails neatly furled.

Rosamund craned to take in the iconic building, striving to concentrate on the view, not the man beside her. Or the fact they were going to be alone together for the foreseeable future.

Excitement warred with worry. When they'd first met it had been much easier, because she'd told herself she hated him.

That didn't last, did it?

Now she felt like she teetered on the brink of something momentous. Because of Fotis.

It didn't make sense because she never let thoughts of any man cloud her judgement. Been there, done that, learnt her lesson. She'd been duped so easily, she didn't trust her thinking around a man who made her feel too much. Even her mother, the person she'd most looked up to, had been taken in by the man she'd married.

Yet it was hard to think of that with Fotis.

Why did you kiss him in a public place, in front of a paparazzo?

Rosamund firmed her mouth and peered again at the scenery.

Past the steep ridge, the other side of the island was more

fertile. Gentle slopes interspersed with ancient stone terraces sprawled down towards a semicircular bay. A village sat on the shore. She saw orchards and a breeze ruffled the grey-green foliage in olive groves.

But what held her attention was a jumble of rocks on a steep hill between the razorback ridge and the village. Late sunlight turned the rubble into blocks of bronze.

The chopper banked and she found herself looking down on a roofless building. And another, a cobblestoned street wending between them. Then the terracotta tiles of a domed Byzantine-style church. Sprawling stone steps that led nowhere. Large trees shivered and swayed as they dropped closer.

'*This* is where you live?'

Fotis nodded, his attention on the instrument panel and the scene before them. 'One of the places. I have a home in Athens but this is my retreat. Easier to keep you safe here than in the city. There's excellent electronic security and any outsiders would be noticed immediately.'

The island was too small to be on the tourist map and any stranger would be obvious. But a deserted town?

They swung around a curve and there, seeming to grow straight up from a sheer cliff, was a long two-storey building, old but clearly renovated. Rows of windows looked towards the sea and the terracotta roof was a blend of old and new tiles.

Fotis flew low over it to land on a crisply painted helipad.

Of course he didn't live anywhere as ordinary as a modern apartment or conventional house. The man cloaked himself in mystery. Even his business was about keeping and decoding secrets. Why not live in a deserted mediaeval town?

'What's the joke?' he asked as she took off her headphones and the sound of the rotors faded.

'You thought I was elitist because I was born in a palace. Yet you live in a...' She surveyed the large building. 'Castle?'

'Abandoned monastery.'

Rosamund couldn't help it, laughter bubbled up.

His winged eyebrows rose but there was a gleam in his eyes that might have been wry amusement. The sight made her stomach do a curious sweep and shimmy motion that had nothing to do with their chopper flight. 'And that's funny because...?'

'You really are reclusive. Like those monks who cut themselves off from the outside world, looking for peace and tranquility. Does anyone else live here?'

'Just me. A couple from the village look after the place.'

So you're going to be alone with him there.

They'd been alone in the Paris house and she'd enjoyed the relative peace, even managed to do a little work. But things had changed. *She'd* changed, become so attuned to him that it was hard to think of anything else.

'I bring some of my team here when we're working on something that requires close collaboration.'

Rosamund didn't know whether to be impressed, jealous, or disturbed that he lived in an eyrie, perched on a rock in the middle of an isolated island.

There were times when she wished she had a bolt-hole where she could truly escape when she needed to concentrate. 'You don't get lonely?' she asked as she undid her seat belt.

'I'm happy with my own company. Anyway, I find company when I want it.'

His voice dropped to a deep note that made her lift her

head to meet his stare. His eyes seemed brighter, his expression intense and she realised what he meant by company.

Women. Sex.

It was as if he'd flicked a switch inside her. Far from being weary from the journey to Greece or distracted by her churning thoughts, she was suddenly hyper-aware. That hooded stare made her breasts grow heavy, heat brewing in that secret feminine place between her legs.

Suddenly all the things she'd been trying *not* to think filled her brain.

Rosamund imagined his gaze holding hers as he drove himself deep inside her, filling her to the brim. Those callused palms stroking her breasts, skimming her thighs and then the place where need throbbed hard and fast. She remembered the taste of his mouth and imagined having the freedom to taste him all over.

She jerked her head around to stare out the side window, nostrils flaring as she dragged air into constrained lungs.

All day they'd skirted around the sexual awareness clotting the air between them.

Her stupid impulse to kiss him at the restaurant had been a mistake. She'd known it but hadn't been able to resist. Had barely been able to resist the temptation of him last night when his murmured invitation to retire early had sent her into a tailspin of longing.

She couldn't understand this man's power.

Like her mother, she had a strong impulsive streak. Like her mother, it had got her into trouble when she was young. But circumstances and the strictures of her royal role meant Rosamund had finally curbed what her father had curtly labelled her waywardness.

At twenty-eight, Rosamund had learnt to think before acting. Yes, setting Ricardo up had been impetuous, but based on sound reasoning. She couldn't stand by and allow him to destroy an innocent's life. Dimitria Politis wouldn't have believed her, if she'd told her about Ricardo's sickening bragging. The girl was besotted and would trust her lover over a woman she didn't know.

But kissing Fotis Mavridis? That had been utterly foolhardy. Because now he was in her mind, in her blood, in a way she'd never experienced before.

The door opened and there he was, well over six feet of impressive masculinity. Her heart gave a silly flutter which she chose to ignore, just as she ignored his outstretched hand and stepped down without help.

It felt like a victory, given how badly she wanted his touch. But she couldn't allow herself to be swept along thoughtlessly.

Control. That was what she'd worked hard to achieve and it had kept her safe for years.

He closed the chopper door behind her. 'This way.'

He led her around the corner of the building, past a huge, spreading tree. On the far side of the space were other buildings in various stages of disrepair, some with empty windows that allowed her to see right through to the stunning views beyond.

'It's not just a monastery is it? It's a whole town.'

'It was. It was abandoned when most islanders left for the city or migrated abroad. A century ago all those terraces and fields were cultivated, supporting a larger population.'

'And there are windmills,' she murmured. 'They're very striking.'

Rosamund was amazed that her voice emerged evenly when there was a riot going on in her body. Tiny detonations of awareness ignited in her blood because he walked so close, shortening his stride to match hers.

Was it any wonder she tried to fill the silence? If they weren't talking, there'd be nothing to keep her from her circling, needy thoughts.

'We've restored one of them.'

The hint of pride in his voice made her want to survey him but she kept her attention on the large door on the far side of the courtyard.

Control, remember?

'We?'

'The residents. We get supplies in from the mainland but it's sensible to be as self-sufficient as possible, besides, it's good to maintain some of the place's heritage.'

She was about to say something about the importance of preserving heritage but they'd reached the door and she'd reached the end of her small talk. It was too much effort.

The door was ornate and imposing but instead of a key, Fotis pressed his palm to a sensor and the door swung wide. 'Welcome to my home, Rosamund.'

The way he said her name, flawlessly yet with just the tiniest hint of an Aegean accent, made her skin tighten. It always did, ever since he'd stopped calling her Princess in a scathing tone. She'd become addicted to the sound of it in that soft, deep rumble. It was one of the things she'd miss when they eventually went their separate ways.

Rosamund swallowed hard and stepped over the threshold.

She wasn't sure what she'd expected of his home but it wasn't this, she realised, as she looked around the spacious foyer and the glimpses into other spaces.

The building was old, its gracious bones clearly visible in the high arched ceilings and thick walls. It might have been tempting to leave the place bare and spartan, or turn it into a showpiece of ultra-modern design.

Instead she was surprised to find it…warm. The proportions were enormous, designed to accommodate large numbers, but the use of soft ochres and cream on the walls softened that. As did the eclectic mix of furniture, reclaimed as well as meticulously craftsman-built.

On one huge wall was a monumental painting. Ochre earth, grey stones, the deep blue of the sea and, bathed in the golden hues of sunset, a row of dilapidated windmills, like battered but still-fierce guardians. The artist had imbued them somehow with a quality that was more human than inanimate.

Drawn, she moved closer, searching for a signature.

As if reading her mind, Fotis said, 'He doesn't sign his work.'

'He doesn't? That's…' She shook her head. 'Unusual. Why?'

'You'll have to ask him that.'

The voice came from right beside her and she made herself focus on the bold brushstrokes rather than the heat dabbling her skin from where he stood so close. Finally his words sank in. 'The artist lives here? On the island?'

She turned, only to be ensnared by those crystalline eyes. Her ribs squeezed around her lungs and her lips parted, eager for air.

Or eager for something else. Another taste of forbidden fruit? It took everything she had to keep her gaze locked on Fotis' eyes, rather than drop to his mouth.

'He does. Tassos is very private about his art. He prefers to keep it to himself. I believe that's not uncommon with some creative people.'

Did Fotis' voice turn challenging, or was that imagination? He couldn't possibly know about her writing. Yet his direct stare made her wonder how much he'd seen.

Rosamund looked again at the painting. 'Is that why he lives here? He sees it as a haven?' Maybe that explained her impression that the rough mountain and the windmills weren't simply starkly beautiful but represented a protective bulwark.

The silence drew out. 'You do see a lot, don't you?' Fotis said in a voice that defied definition. 'This place has always been a haven. Generations upon generations lived here. They even moved their town up onto this hill centuries ago, to protect themselves from marauding pirates.'

'Pirates? Really?' It was easier to focus on colourful history than the awareness zinging through her blood, because of a man who was only beside her because he'd promised Leon he'd keep her safe.

'Really. They were dire times, but the cliffs and high walls kept the people safe most of the time.' He paused. 'Now there are no pirates, but it's still a haven.'

For him too? Rosamund desperately wanted to know. She wanted to understand him. What had made him a recluse? What had given him the drive to build a multibillion-dollar business? Why, in repose, was his expression often so stern?

But if she quizzed him, the quid pro quo meant he'd have every right to question her.

She turned, and just as she'd known, he was scrutinising her, not the artwork. His brow furrowed as if she intrigued him. It was arousing and terrifying, having that fiercely insightful mind turned on her.

Almost as arousing as the idea of them together, naked, the way she'd been imagining.

Without a word, he beckoned for her to follow him, leading her up the wide staircase. At the end of an upstairs corridor he opened a door. 'This is yours. I'm next door if you need anything.'

The room was simple but pure luxury. Windows down one wall gave spectacular views towards the sea and through an open door she glimpsed a well-appointed bathroom.

Another luxurious, empty suite.

Another lonely, empty night.

Rosamund paused in the doorway. It struck her suddenly, how much time she spent alone. How she ached for...more. Ached for *him*.

She liked solitude, needed it for her work, but still there was a yearning inside her, a yearning so powerful it bubbled up, an unstoppable force. She wondered if he could read it in her face.

'Rosamund? What is it?'

Her pulse quickened. Was she really going to do this? After all the effort she'd put into being sensible?

Part of her couldn't believe it. Another part screamed at her to hurry up. Once that inner voice, the impulsive one, had dominated. But years learning caution had stifled it so now she didn't know whether to trust it.

'I do need something.' How glorious it was, how freeing, to admit it.

He stepped before her. 'What is it you need?'

'You, Fotis.' She put her hand to his darkly stubbled jaw, tracing its strong lines, feeling his solid heat under her hand with something like relief. 'I need you.'

CHAPTER NINE

HE WAS SILENT so long, she wondered if he hadn't heard her.
Oh, he heard. Those eyes blazed so hot they scorched her.
'What, exactly, are you suggesting?'

What part of *I need you*, didn't he understand? She hadn't imagined his implicit invitation to share his bed last night, had she? No, his meaning had been potently clear.

She angled her chin up. 'You and me together. Naked.' She watched a pulse throb at his temple, felt his muscles move as he swallowed.

'Is this guilt talking?'

'What do you mean?'

He nodded towards his arm. 'Because I got hurt. Your way of making amends? Paying me back?'

Rosamund dropped her hand and stepped away, suddenly trembling. She *did* feel guilty that he'd been injured because of her. More than guilty. Thinking of him in pain was hard. But this was something else.

Suddenly what had felt so simple had become tainted.

'You think I use sex as a payment? A way of balancing the books?' Her stomach rolled so much she felt almost sick. Over the years people had tried to make her feel cheap but it was rare they succeeded. But now... 'Strangely enough, I've never propositioned one of my bodyguards before.'

'I didn't mean—'

'It's okay, Fotis. I know what you meant.' He imagined she used her body as a commodity.

'No! You don't.' His voice was strident, a far cry from his usual even tones. He ploughed his hand through his hair, leaving it ruffled and ridiculously appealing. She hated that she noticed. 'I'm not insulting you. I thought you were feeling sorry for me. You shouldn't feel guilty about what happened when it's not your fault. It was mine for letting down my guard.' He took a deep breath that lifted his powerful chest. 'I should never have let you leave the premises with me. You could have been hurt.'

To her amazement his voice was uneven.

'You thought I was offering pity sex?'

Those broad shoulders lifted. 'It's a possibility.'

Rosamund shook her head. 'It was my decision to leave the party with you. You gave your professional advice and I ignored it, so it was *my* fault. I regret what happened to you and I *do* feel guilty. But that's got nothing to do with this.'

'No?' He folded his arms, making her wish he'd move away from her doorway so she could go inside and shut the door behind her.

'No!'

'Good.'

'Good? What do you mean?' Somehow she'd lost track of the conversation. Why had she thought telling Fotis she wanted him would make things easy? Nothing had been easy between them.

'Two adults acting on pure sexual attraction sounds perfect to me.'

Her mind must have slowed because it took a second for his meaning to sink in. When it did it was like a bomb exploding inside, reigniting the desire his earlier words had doused. 'Perfect?'

She didn't think she'd ever had perfect in her life. But the thrill she got just from being close to this man and the confidence he exuded, made her suspect being with him could come close. His eyes glittered with an unholy heat that made her knees loosen.

'There's just one thing,' he added. 'I don't do long-term relationships.' His gaze dropped to her mouth and it was as if he'd drawn a line of heat along her lips then down to her breasts and further, deep into her womb. 'I'm not after emotional attachment. I don't want that. If there's any danger of you getting emotionally involved—'

'No. There's not.' She almost wished there was. But her experiences had soured that possibility. Romantic dreams were for innocents. Rosamund was a pragmatist now. 'All I'm hoping for is mind-blowing sex.'

'That,' he said with a slow-growing smile that twisted her insides in knots, 'I can deliver.'

He moved so swiftly, he took her by surprise, hoisting her into his arms and up against his chest. She was surrounded by hard male and heat so intense it seemed almost feverish. She planted one hand on his chest, pleased to feel his heart thudding as fast as her own.

He turned his back on her room. 'Fotis?'

'What is it?' He stopped, looking down with a frown. 'You want to wait?'

Held securely in that iron-hard embrace, she *felt* his urgency and saw it reflected in his features. She almost smiled her relief. 'No! I just wondered why you're walking away from a perfectly good bed.'

He moved swiftly along the hallway, shouldering his way through another door, and she marvelled at the intriguing feeling of weightlessness as he carried her so easily. 'Mine has a stock of condoms in the bedside table.'

Her breath snagged at the febrile glaze of desire in his eyes. She'd only seen him fully clothed but she had an excellent imagination. He was a tall man and well-built. She suspected that naked he'd be imposing. He certainly was in her taunting, erotic dreams. She wanted to watch him roll on a condom while he watched her with that naked hunger in his eyes.

'Then what are we waiting for?'

A smile hooked up the corner of his mouth and something inside her dissolved. Serious or disapproving he was stunning. But amused and approachable he was downright dangerous.

Deliciously, temptingly dangerous. She wanted to lose herself in that smile. In his arms, his body, and not surface for a long, long time.

With an ease that spoke of impressive strength, he lowered her slowly to her feet. Their bodies brushed together, centimetre by centimetre, the friction teasing and delighting. She swayed against him, hands going automatically to his shirt buttons. She started at the top while he reefed the shirt free of his trousers.

The top of his shirt gaped wide and her knuckles brushed hot flesh and crisp chest hair over tight muscles. She looked down, following the narrow trail of dark hair descending from his chest over glowing, golden skin.

She'd been so right about his body, she decided as she pushed his shirt off with a silent sigh of appreciation.

He had broad shoulders and the leanly honed muscles of an athlete. As she stroked down his body those tight muscles twitched under her touch. As if she had power over him.

As he did over her. Just the sight of Fotis, half-naked,

had turned the needy place between her legs butter-soft. Her breasts swelled and low inside she ached.

Her fingers reached his trousers. His belt. She wanted...

'My turn.'

His voice was raw gravel and only added to her arousal. She looked up and there she saw the same desperation she felt. It slammed into her, an affirmation so powerful she couldn't remember ever feeling so good.

And they'd barely started.

His hands rose to her shoulder straps, then slowly down, skimming the fabric that crossed above her décolletage, then lower, feathering the material that covered her breasts.

Her hum of approval sounded more like a growl as she pressed into his hands, squeezing her thighs tight together against a tide of liquid pleasure as he cupped and squeezed her breasts. She'd never been more grateful that a bra was impossible in this dress.

'Do you have any idea how hard it's been, keeping my hands off you? Especially in that dress. Did you wear it to torment me?'

'Of course not,' she groaned as he weighed her breasts in his palms then followed the fabric lower, to where the two wide bands of fabric parted, leaving an upside-down V of flesh bare at her midriff. His fingertips stroked her skin and even that felt like erotic overload.

'The dress is perfectly respectable,' she croaked. The skirt was knee-length, and while the straps revealed more than usual of her back, the bodice was modest but for that small triangle of bare flesh above her waist.

But appearances lied. The wide crossed straps covered her breasts fully but once over her shoulders they narrowed, crossing over her back before circling her waist to tie at the front. Everything essential was covered but undo that tie and yank the straps...

She'd worn it because it made her feel bold and attractive. Defiant.

'So you were making a point for the cameras, not me, with all that sultry sexiness.'

She put her hands on his, intending to drag them back to her aching breasts. But then he spanned her waist in what felt deliciously like possessiveness and she confessed, 'Maybe I dressed for you too.'

Not to tease, but because she'd wanted, badly, to have him look at her like an attractive woman one more time, not like someone he'd simply sworn to protect.

'I'm glad. I approve.'

His teeth flashed in a feral smile as he grasped her hips and yanked her to him.

Rosamund's mind went blank as she registered the thick length of his erection pressing against her abdomen. Then she rose on her toes, grabbing the hard muscles at his shoulders, and ground her pelvis against him.

So good. So very, very good.

Eyelids at half-mast, she saw him grit his teeth, a man on the edge. Excitement spiked.

'You have three seconds to undo that dress before I damage it when I rip it off you.'

For a shocking second she toyed with the idea of calling his bluff. But she loved seeing Fotis teetering on the brink of control. She intended to wear this dress again, often.

Before this, sex had been enjoyable but never thrilling. She discovered she liked thrilling.

Leaning back, she swiftly undid the discreet bow at her waist then dragged down the wide straps covering her chest. The bodice dropped, leaving her naked from the waist up.

Rosamund didn't understand Greek but she didn't need to. His whispered words were heartfelt and made her stand taller so her breasts jutted towards him. His husky voice and the avid gleam in his eyes made her feel like a goddess.

But when he stroked his hands, feather-light, over her bare breasts, she was all woman, surging forward into his hold, grabbing at his shoulders for balance as he wrought the most incredible sensations in her needy body.

'Fotis.'

It sounded shockingly like a plea and she didn't care. Nothing mattered but the promise of carnal pleasure. This, between them, was more profound, more intense than anything she'd experienced.

He bent to suck at her breast and her head arched back in rapture, fiery trails of sensation coursing through her.

Clamping his head to her breast she reached down between them, fumbling with his belt. As magnificent as this was, she needed more. She needed everything.

More Greek words, this time a growl, and suddenly she was at arm's length from him, gasping at the interruption.

'Take your dress off.'

She blinked up at him, trying to decipher his words. His accent was suddenly so pronounced it took a second to realise he spoke in English. Or maybe it was the rush of blood in her head, affecting her hearing.

He was already stripping off his shoes and socks as she kicked off her sandals, undid the zip and pushed the dress to the floor.

The sight of Fotis in that moment was something she'd never forget, even if she lived to be a hundred.

Hair tousled, bare feet planted wide, hands frozen in the act of yanking his belt undone, his chest heaved mightily as if he struggled to drag air into that spectacular body.

But it was his eyes above all that entranced her. Eyes that glittered with a sharp possessive hunger mixed with something like awe.

She knew the feeling. She'd never seen a man so stunningly beautiful. Never wanted the way she wanted him. Never felt desire so untamed it felt primal.

For a second Rosamund shivered as something like fear coursed through her.

But she'd spent her adult life being cautious. She wanted, needed just this once, to follow her instinct. To forget responsibility and expectations and just *be*.

Holding his gaze, she hooked her fingers into her underwear, dragging the lace and damp silk down to drop onto the floor.

Fotis swallowed, the movement jerky as his eyes ate her up. Then with a few quick movements, the last of his clothes hit the floor and he stepped free of them.

She'd been so right. The man was stunning. Every line and dip, every muscled curve and hard plane impressive. So impressive she felt a quiver of nerves at the thought of accommodating his rampant erection.

Nerves and anticipation. Her fingers flexed. She wanted to explore, touch and taste and discover all his secrets.

He leaned across and yanked open a drawer in the bedside cabinet, withdrawing a box of condoms. She took a half-step forward, about to offer to help, when he shook his head. 'On the bed,' he said, his voice rough. 'Please.'

He looked as strung out as she felt, and she wondered if he too felt on the edge of climax.

Just from watching him undress, and the feel of his mouth at her breast!

She wobbled her way to the bed then climbed up to lie on her back, watching as he stroked on the condom. Each movement of his hand felt like a phantom caress between her thighs. She twitched, shifting her weight and opening her legs, needing his body against hers, *in* hers as she'd never needed any man.

His gaze caressed her body and she felt it as surely as she'd felt his hands on her waist, hips and breasts. She licked her lips and willed herself not to beg.

A couple of strides and he was at the base of the bed, but instead of following her onto it, he reached for her ankles and tugged her sharply down its length. The move was so abrupt he was kneeling on the floor between her knees before she registered him moving. Another tug and her buttocks settled on the edge of the bed. She wriggled her hips to bring herself closer to all that glorious heat and hardness.

'Rosa.'

The diminutive startled her, but it sounded so right in that harsh sandpaper voice. Something behind her ribs loosened abruptly. As if a pinched nerve suddenly eased, leaving her limp and basking in unfamiliar approval.

Instinctively she reached for him and he captured her hands, pressing kisses to first one palm then the other, ratcheting up her eagerness. That loosening intensified as tenderness welled.

Fotis released her, but instead of easing his tall frame above hers, he sank low, pushing her thighs wide with his shoulders, his breath hot against her most private place.

She was already shaking her head. 'No, Fotis. I'm too close.'

'Good. I want to taste you as you come.'

The words sent her arousal skyrocketing and that was before he nuzzled her. Unerringly he found her pleasure point with a slow lick that made her arch off the bed.

'But I want—'

'I know you do, *asteri mou*, and I'll give you everything you want. Later. I promise.'

Shining eyes held hers as he kissed her and it was all she could do not to explode as excitement and carnal pleasure melded with something unexpected. Stunned, she just had time to register a wave of poignant emotion. Then what he did with his mouth scrambled all thought.

Needy hands speared his thick hair, holding him close. Then his fingers were on her, circling, exploring, insinuating into slick heat.

Her eyes must've closed because white light pulsed behind her eyelids in time with every thrust of his fingers and each caress of his mouth. Her hips rose, seeking, and he spread his other hand beneath her, angling her higher.

Rosamund scrabbled to regain control but was far too late. The splashes of white light were edged now with golden sparks, sparks igniting deep within.

Stunned at the intensity of sensation, she snapped her eyes open to find him watching her. 'That's it, Rosa,' he growled, his breath hot against tenderest flesh and his short beard scraping her inner thighs as she clamped her legs around him. 'Come for me. Now.'

As if on command, she convulsed, overwhelmed by a peak of pleasure that went on and on and on. Still he caressed her, as if needing to ensure she lost all control. She couldn't breathe, couldn't think, could only ride crest after crest of jubilation.

She was boneless, shaky with aftershocks and utterly euphoric. Never had a man taken her to such heights.

Another caress made her shudder, overloaded with bliss. But it took his withdrawal to lift her heavy eyelids.

'Thank you,' she croaked as he rose between her legs. 'That was amazing.'

He was amazing with his generosity and unstinting care for her pleasure.

'You're welcome.' His mouth hitched up in a smile that was positively devilish. 'But wait, there's more.'

'Good, because I need you.'

Despite the incredible orgasm, she felt a hollow ache inside. And despite clenching internal muscles, the need wasn't just physical. She wanted the intimacy of being heart to heart with this man. It might be an illusion but she craved more than physical satiation.

Callused fingertips ran down her thighs and along her calves then he lifted her legs up, draping her ankles over his shoulders as he leaned towards her.

It wasn't what she'd expected but when she felt the heavy nudge of his erection at her core it made sense. She felt open to him, completely dominated by his larger body, and it excited her.

'Okay?'

'Absolutely okay.'

He leaned closer, nudging her and pushing in a fraction. She felt her eyes widen as she stretched.

He planted his hands on the bed either side of her and bowed forward, lips skimming her breast. 'I thought this might be easier for you until you get accustomed...'

To the size of him. Rosamund nodded. She'd known he was big but...

Teeth closed around her nipple in the tiniest nip as he pressed further, the pressure so right. Still he slid deeper.

'Breathe, Rosa.' She opened her eyes to see him frowning down at her. 'Are you all right?'

She nodded, circling her hips, inviting him further. 'Fill me, Fotis. I want all of you.'

She wanted to possess him, experience his climax, feel

him lose control, just for her. She was so hungry for him, it shocked her.

Holding her gaze, he thrust long and slow, impaling himself so deep it felt like he'd reached her heart.

For a breath neither moved. Then she squeezed him and was rewarded by a flicker of those long dark eyelashes.

It would be easy to feel overwhelmed by his sheer physical presence. Instead she was excited. She knew her own power, squeezing again as she gently raked her fingernails down his torso, feeling him shudder.

'Rosa!' His hoarse voice was somewhere between a warning and a plea.

'What's the matter, Fotis?' She gasped as he withdrew and surged back slowly, finding a deliciously sensitive spot that made her writhe. 'You can dish it out but you can't take it?'

For answer he withdrew then bucked hard, so hard she'd never felt anything so perfect. He did it again and again, his slow precision driving her wild. Even as her rough cries of pleasure filled the air she needed to bring him undone.

She reached down to where his thighs slapped against her buttocks with every hungry thrust. Questing fingers found his sac and slowly squeezed.

There was a rough gasp as he arched high before taking her again, his movements jagged.

'Don't.' He pulled her hand away, his gentleness at odds with the feral gleam in his eyes. 'I can't last like that.'

'Then don't.' Her voice was unsteady. 'I want you to lose yourself.' Much as she'd rejoiced in her own climax, she wanted to be with Fotis when he reached that same point.

Their gazes held and she wondered what he saw in hers. Carefully he eased her legs down and she wrapped them around his hips. Now he lay over her, taking his weight on his elbows, his chest against hers, the friction of his hair-roughened chest against her nipples delicious torture.

Slowly he moved, retreating then surging. 'All right?'

'More than all right.'

She rose to meet the next thrust, matching his rhythm, drawn by instinct and the desire to give him the joy he'd given her. But somehow, the needs of her own body grew clamorous. She felt the wave rise, unstoppable. 'I can't—'

His mouth took hers, gently at first, then deeper, mimicking the sensual thrusts of their bodies.

Rosamund felt the ripples begin, then he came alive in an urgent explosion of movement, bucking frantically and pushing them both over the edge into ecstasy. The feel of him pulsing, losing himself deep inside her, was indescribably satisfying.

She swallowed his roar of completion, feeling her own blend of triumph, exquisite physical pleasure and, as she gradually came back to herself, tenderness for this man.

Her arms wrapped around him and her heart squeezed. He nuzzled the sensitive curve of her neck as he slumped over her, still trembling from his climax.

Even spent, his presence inside her took some getting used to.

Because he felt so good. Too good?

Rosamund felt such a profound connection. Her need for him to reach ecstasy had been more than a generous urge. It had been a necessity.

She'd wanted him to have everything he'd given her and more. Greedily, she'd wanted to be with him through it all.

She was discriminating about lovers and it was a very long time since she'd been with anyone. Yet, as she stroked the hot silky skin of his back, and felt a glow in her chest, she wondered if she'd just made a huge mistake.

Fotis lifted his head, heavy-lidded eyes meeting hers, then slid his arms around her and rolled onto his back so she was draped over him.

'Better,' he murmured, kissing her languidly.

Rosamund lost her train of thought.

CHAPTER TEN

Fotis approached the old windmill, a breeze riffling his shirt as he topped the ridgeline.

The door was propped open and Rosamund sat on the stone block that wedged it wide. She was writing, her attention on the notebook open on her lap. A broad-brimmed hat lay discarded on the ground. Even in the shade, her rose-gold hair seemed to catch the light.

Her legs were stretched out, casually crossed at the ankles. Fotis thought of how she'd locked those slim, strong limbs around him this morning as she urged him deeper, faster, harder.

He paused and drew a slow breath.

She wore a crimson cotton dress with narrow shoulder straps that left her arms and shoulders bare. He knew she wore nothing beneath it except a pair of skimpy, lace underpants. Lying on the rumpled bed, he'd watched her dress, only just restraining himself from reaching for her again, because she'd declared she needed fresh air after spending so long in bed.

He thought he'd done well, not mentioning that she'd been the one to disrupt his offer to prepare breakfast, her seeking, stroking hands revealing that it wasn't food she'd been hungry for. Inevitably she'd woken the beast in him and they'd stayed in bed for another hour.

Their affair had lasted for weeks and still they were voracious for each other. Just a look, a touch, a half-smile, and nothing mattered but satisfying that hunger. By mutual consent, and while Ricardo was still at large, there'd been no mention of her leaving.

Fotis had found himself working less than he usually did, only when she was busy on her laptop. His business ran well and he trusted his senior staff but soon, surely, he'd have to pull back from her and return to his well-ordered life.

Yet for hours the image of her, lifting the cherry-red dress over her head and letting it waft down over her almost-naked body, had made work impossible.

Besides, despite the safety of this isolated island with its state-of-the-art security monitoring, he couldn't rest easy if she wasn't near. Every day she explored, sometimes with him and sometimes ostensibly on her own. But Fotis always ensured either he or a trusted local was close enough to step in if danger threatened.

He wouldn't allow anything bad to happen to her.

Because you gave your word to her brother? Or because you can't stand the thought of her being hurt?

The answer was both. Yet his visceral reaction to the idea of her in danger had little to do with Leon or their deal.

Nor was his response based solely on sex. The carnal link between them was incredibly strong. But more than that Fotis *liked* Rosamund.

She wasn't afraid to challenge him and he enjoyed the give-and-take of their discussions, even their disagreements. Time and again she'd made him consider things in a new light. She was living proof that he wasn't always right and that first impressions could be wrong. A valuable reminder for a man in his field. In his work he'd never dream of jumping to conclusions, yet he'd done that with her.

'Are you hungry? I brought food.'

She lifted her head, expression brimming with a delight that made his heart thud. Her slow curling smile and the pleasure in her grey-blue eyes drew heat through his tightening chest, down past his belly and into his groin.

'Sounds wonderful. I'm famished.'

'So am I.' Not merely for food.

Fotis closed the space between them and dropped a kiss to her parted lips.

Immediately need rose. Her response was as instantaneous as it was generous. She palmed his jaw, leaning up towards him, and he felt her hunger. It matched his. For a deeper taste. For the feel of their bodies against each other. For the sweet bliss of communion.

But he pulled back, making himself straighten, his lungs working like bellows and every muscle protesting. Because he was determined for once not to tumble immediately into sex.

He'd known alluring women, enjoyed his time with enough of them. Yet none had had this effect on him. Weeks it had been since they'd become lovers, and in that time his desire for her, his *hunger*, had only intensified.

He needed... What? To understand this link between them. To identify the nebulous feelings she stirred. They were unsettling to a man who'd spent his life determinedly alone.

He swung the backpack off his shoulders and onto the ground. 'I've brought cheese and fresh bread—'

'*Yiayia* Irini's bread?'

He nodded, smiling as her face lit with greedy eagerness. 'Tassos brought some up especially for you.'

Because Rosamund had developed a weakness for the flavoursome bread and nothing, it seemed, was too much effort for the locals where she was concerned. She'd visited the village early during her stay and found the elderly woman removing a loaf of bread she'd baked from the old communal oven. The oven was only used by a few now, but some of the traditional ways hadn't died.

Naturally Irini had offered the visitor a taste of her loaf, using her smattering of English. A bond had sprung up between the princess and the tiny, sharp-eyed matriarch of the village. Not just with Irini. He'd lost count of the people who'd spent time with Rosamund and liked her.

He liked her. More than he'd thought possible.

He looked away from her shining eyes as he opened the pack. 'There are olives and tomatoes. Plus I've got a bottle of local wine and apricot tart for dessert.'

'It sounds like a feast,' she said as she closed her notebook and put it aside.

Fotis noted with pleasure that she hadn't snapped it shut the moment she saw him, like she used to do. She was relaxed, anticipation dancing her eyes.

He'd seen her at VIP functions that featured world-famous wines and exquisite gourmet delicacies. Yet here she was, licking her lips over rustic bread, tomatoes warm from the sun and a light wine that was tasty but would never feature on a list of must-have vintages.

Rosamund was anything but elitist.

He pulled out a rug and spread it out while she delved into the rucksack, busily setting out the food. She grabbed a knife. 'I'll cut the bread and the tomatoes if you'll open the wine.'

As Fotis uncorked the bottle and poured it, he tried to

imagine any of his previous lovers enjoying such a simple picnic. He couldn't.

The women in his life hadn't been socialites, since he had an inbuilt hatred of the species. They were all intelligent, attractive women, not searching for a man to give them a life of luxury. Yet he couldn't picture any of them here on this superb but wild mountain, avidly eyeing his humble picnic.

He handed her some wine and she leaned in to brush her lips against his, lingering for a tantalising moment that tested his resolve, before withdrawing. She tasted of the sea breeze and cinnamon, and something deeply sensual that was unique to her. Something that made him want to lean in for more.

Blue eyes twinkled. She knew exactly how much he wanted her. 'Thanks for hiking up with the food, Fotis.' She raised her glass. '*Yassou.*'

He lifted his own in salute. '*Yassou*, Rosa.'

He loved her reaction to the intimate nickname. The hint of a flush across her throat and the glow of pleasure in her beautiful eyes. It made him want...

Fotis swallowed a mouthful of crisp wine then reached for an olive, breaking their locked gazes.

'I have a question.' It had been on his mind for weeks, that incident in Paris that had set the seal on his initial negative opinion. An opinion that didn't fit the woman he knew.

She tilted her head. 'Go on.'

'Tell me about the dress in the Paris boutique. The red one you rejected.'

At first he'd imagined her reaction was simply selfishness. Now he knew better. Her manner at the boutique was at odds with the way she dealt with other people. Completely at odds with how she interacted with the villagers here.

Rosamund paused in the act of laying a tomato slice on

a piece of bread. A tiny frown line appeared in the centre of her forehead as she took her time adding another slice. 'What do you want to know?'

He hated the wariness in her voice and how her lush mouth pinched at the corners. But he wanted more from her, more than sexual gratification. He hungered to *know* her. He told himself it was a form of self-protection to understand her, yet an inner voice warned he was in dangerous territory.

So be it. He'd crossed a line with this woman and he couldn't go back. He *needed* to understand her.

'It wasn't just any dress, was it? It upset you and you weren't yourself, the way you handled the situation.'

'In what way?'

'You were abrupt. Terse.' At the time he'd thought that was typical of her, that she was spoiled and angry when she didn't get exactly what she wanted. The way his mother had been when things didn't work out to her satisfaction, even the smallest things. 'That's unusual for you. You make such an effort to put people at ease, particularly those who aren't your social equals.'

Her eyebrows arched high. 'Don't be a snob, Fotis. Just because my father was a king doesn't mean I'm superior to someone who makes beautiful clothing, or who can ferry me safely through peak hour Paris traffic.'

As if to emphasise that she'd made her point, she took a big bite of bread and tomato.

He watched her chew vigorously then swallow, but without any sign of enjoyment, as if the conversation had tainted the taste of the food. Her eyes flashed with annoyance yet still he couldn't drag his eyes away. Her vibrant energy was captivating.

'I agree. And I know that's how you feel. Which is why I

want to understand what distressed you.' For she *had* been distressed, he'd realised.

She looked away to where the indigo sea met the horizon. 'Maybe I was annoyed at being lumbered with an unwanted bodyguard.'

'I'm sure you were.' She hadn't held back with him. He'd been surprised at how much he'd enjoyed the cut and thrust of their battle of wills. 'But I know you'd never take that anger out on women who were just doing their job.'

Her head swung around abruptly. Was that dismay in her eyes? 'You think I was rude to them?'

'Not rude. Emphatic. They were clearly disappointed.'

Slowly she nodded, then looked down at the food in her hand as if wondering how it got there. She put it down and reached for her wine, sipping slowly. Her mouth curled wryly.

'You don't miss much, do you? You must be very good at your job, searching out secrets and hiding them.'

He said nothing, just reached for another olive and popped it into his mouth. Eventually she sighed and took another sip of wine. 'Okay, I'll tell you.' Her gaze snagged his. 'But it's private.'

'I won't tell anyone. Your secret will be safe with me.'

'It's not really my secret, but still...' She paused as if weighing something up. 'I feel like I'm the one who's always sharing with you. You already know I had an experience like your friend Dimi's. You know why I did what I did in New York.'

'And you want to know something private about me.' It was a statement, not a question.

She spread her hands wide. 'Fair's fair. You don't *need* to know about the dress to keep me safe, do you?'

Fotis expected an instinctive internal protest at the idea

of sharing anything personal. Instead he found himself nodding. Whatever he told her, he knew it wouldn't go further. He trusted Rosamund and not just with his body, he realised.

Another first. He could count on the fingers of one hand the people he trusted completely.

'Okay.' He piled tomato and cheese onto a slice of bread and lifted it. 'Tell me about the dress and I'll tell you something private about myself.'

Her eyes rounded, as if surprised by his agreement, yet still she didn't leap at the chance to pry into his secrets. That set her apart from many he'd known.

The more time they spent together, the more he realised she was unique.

She leaned back against the doorjamb. The breeze lifted a few strands of richly coloured hair. His gaze traced the tender curve of her ear, the slim line of her throat and the tiny frown gathered across the bridge of her nose.

She looked…endearing. Sensual and alluring but without any hint of artifice. Affection stirred.

'You didn't recognise the dress?'

Her sharp tone punctured his thoughts. 'Should I have?'

Her mouth turned down, not in her naturally sexy pout but in definite distaste. 'The photo of my mother at the gala. The huge one projected on the massive wall as you entered.' Her eyes met his. 'The famous one with her wearing a dress that looked like it was about to slide off her at any moment.'

That dress. The one that revealed the maximum flesh while still being arguably decent. He pursed his lips in a silent whistle. 'They made a replica for you to wear to the gala?'

His larynx tightened, turning his voice into a growl at the thought of Rosa wearing such a dress where anyone other than he could see her.

Great. Possessive now as well as protective and curious. Where are you heading with this, Mavridis?

She inclined her head.

He scowled. Rosa was a princess, not a movie star or model. Surely that was—'Who arranged it?' But he had the answer. He'd heard her snap out the name. 'Antoine Gaudreau? He organised the event?'

'No!' The word shot out sharply and Rosamund paused to modulate her tone. 'He wasn't the event's organiser, but yes, he arranged the dress.'

'Without consulting you?'

'That's right.'

Fotis' eyes glowed with a martial light. 'I'm glad you didn't wear it.'

'You are?' She tilted her head, frowning. 'Others thought it was a good idea.'

'The women who'd made it? Of course they'd like you to parade it and advertise their work. You'd have looked stunning.'

The thought of wearing the outfit still made her flesh crawl, so she was astonished to discover how much she wanted to look stunning for this man.

It was unsettling. The last time she'd deliberately dressed to impress a guy she'd been seventeen and giddy with her first romantic infatuation.

'Yet you're glad I didn't wear it. Why?'

Was that discomfort in Fotis' expression? 'It's the sort of dress a woman wears for her lover. The thought of you wearing it in public, for everyone to slaver over...' He shook his head.

Pleasure buzzed low in her body. How could she not enjoy his protectiveness and that hint of possessiveness?

For however long this affair lasted, she knew she'd revel in both. She refused to ponder why that was, when she'd spent so long carving out the right to make her own decisions.

With Fotis everything felt different. Another man's protectiveness, certainly another man's possessiveness, would irk her and feel constricting. With him she felt only a warm glow. Briefly she wondered if that was anything like how it felt to be cherished. Then she pushed the idea aside.

'That's exactly why I couldn't wear it.' She'd felt physically ill when they'd shown it to her. 'I'm not ashamed of my sexuality, but I'm not interested in being objectified.'

'Your mother—'

'My mother was barely seventeen when she wore that to the premiere of her first film, and it wasn't her choice.'

She saw Fotis' eyes widen.

'You didn't know? She was just sixteen when Gaudreau *discovered* her and gave her a small part in the film he was shooting. She and her parents were in a village near where the film was being made. By the time it was in post-production he'd decided to make her a star. Or at least a sexy starlet.' Her lip curled. 'He took her under his wing, had her live with him so he could *nurture her talent*.'

She watched Fotis' expression darken, instantly understanding the euphemism for what it was. The famous director had been a controlling predator.

'But her parents! If she told them—'

Rosamund shook her head. 'They traded their daughter for money. Everything she earned on the first films went straight to them. She was young and inexperienced and she *was* excited at the idea of acting. Until she found out the whole of what he wanted from her.'

Her throat closed as she remembered her mother telling her this. Not seeking sympathy, but as a warning about those who preyed on vulnerable young people, particularly women. 'She tried to leave several times, only to be told that if she did he'd sue her parents for breach of contract and ruin them.'

Yet, even knowing that terrible truth about her mother's early career, Rosamund had fallen for another sort of predator in her teens. She hadn't seen the parallels until it was too late. She could only guess how difficult it had been for her mother to be so frank about the abuse she'd endured. Every time she thought about it, Rosamund hated herself for being duped, as if it were a betrayal of her mother's trust.

She was only glad her mother hadn't been alive to witness her mistake. Though if she'd lived maybe things would have been different.

It was easier to think about the red dress. 'Gaudreau knew she'd upstage the star of the film wearing that dress. It made her a household name. Which boosted his career too, since he controlled hers. At least in the beginning.'

What was it with the women in her family and controlling men? First her mother, who'd taken years to find her feet and build a career separate from that loathsome old man. Then, when she was at the pinnacle of her career, she'd fallen for a handsome prince. Too late she'd discovered that while he lusted after the sexy screen siren, he was jealous of her easy charisma and popularity, continually finding fault with his vivacious, charming wife.

Then Rosamund. After her mother's death, her father had become ever more watchful and disapproving, decreeing what she could wear and whom she could meet. Was it any wonder she'd fallen for a handsome, laughing man who played on her need for love? Both men had used her for their own ends.

Was it any wonder she refused to be used anymore? Or that trust came hard?

'So, you see, I couldn't have worn it. That would have been a betrayal of my mother. Gaudreau was just trying to stir interest in those early films, the ones they made together. He wanted to make the event about himself.'

Warmth closed around her hand and she looked down to see Fotis' fingers curling around hers. As ever, she was struck by how well they fitted together, as if made for each other despite their disparity in size.

'I do see, and I'm sorry I misinterpreted the situation. Your mother would be proud of you.'

'I…' She shrugged, suddenly finding it hard to speak. Her mum had been her rock and Rosamund had felt adrift for so long after her early death. She still felt her loss.

Remarkably, it seemed Fotis guessed some of what she felt for he nodded. 'She raised a remarkable woman. Caring but no pushover. Fiery but clever and determined. I can't believe I ever thought you a spoiled socialite.'

His words stunned her. Their physical intimacy had changed their relationship into one of ease and respect. But there was still so much they didn't know about each other. Yet here he was, talking about her in terms that made her suddenly eager heart shudder open.

Inevitably, Rosamund thought of her mother, the only one who'd ever praised her like that.

Fotis might have read her mind. 'Here's to Juliette Bernard.'

'To my beautiful mum.'

The fruity wine trickled down her throat and spread with it a sense of peace. Maybe because, for the first time, she'd spoken unreservedly about the woman who meant so much to her.

Because Fotis understood. His anger when he heard what Gaudreau had done and his approval of her mum and herself felt like balm spread on unhealed wounds.

Over the years her father had twisted her mother's character into something negative. Enthusiasm was described as heedless passion. Generosity became recklessness. Warmth and charisma turned into undisciplined and unrefined behaviour. The very virtues that had attracted him, and won over his people, became character flaws he'd been determined to extinguish in his daughter.

Rosamund turned to the man beside her, who still held her hand clasped in his. His brow was furrowed in thought, his mouth flat as he stared over the vast Aegean.

If he'd wondered about her, it couldn't be nearly as much as she'd pondered him.

He fascinated her and with every day her curiosity rose. Fotis Mavridis wasn't the man she'd first thought, at least not all the way through. He could be harsh and forbidding. He was ruthless and capable, breathtakingly so. She remembered the efficiency with which he'd disabled her attacker in France, ignoring his own injuries as he kept her safe.

But he was thoughtful and generous. Their lovemaking was a revelation, his passion and tenderness unlocking something deep within her that made her want to know everything about him.

He'd happily connected with disadvantaged teenagers in a city slum, even offering one a remarkable opportunity for the future. Her visits to the village here had elicited stories about his generosity. Not just his ability to fund infrastructure, but his genuine involvement in the community.

Tassos, who'd been born on the island, had served in the military with Fotis and lost half his leg while on duty. According to *Yiayia* Irini, it was Fotis who'd dragged him out of his depression and funded extra therapy for him when he got his prosthetic leg. Later he'd offered him a job as an analyst. Now the man was rebuilding his life, working for Fotis and preparing to marry.

'What are you thinking about, Rosa? You look miles away. Is it your mother?'

She shook her head. 'A little. It's good to talk about her. There's no one else I can talk with about her, other than Lucie.' Her father had never wanted to reminisce and Leon had barely known her, for all they'd technically been one family.

She turned, gaze colliding with sea-bright eyes, and a quiver of sensation snaked through her. Desire mixed with a longing that wasn't merely physical. And something else too, delight at this open conversation, sharing in a way she couldn't remember doing before.

'Actually I was thinking what an enigma you are. I know some things about you.' She ticked off her fingers. 'You like your coffee black and strong. You have eclectic tastes in music. Everything from rembetiko,' a Greek style she'd never heard of until she came here, 'to classical. From jazz to hip-hop.'

She knew his dedication to keeping fit, running or using his indoor pool and huge gym, complete with climbing wall. She knew how his hands felt on her hips as she rode him to pleasure. How his deep voice turned deliciously rough when he gasped out her name as ecstasy took him.

Rosamund swallowed. 'I know when you give your word you keep it.' He'd promised to protect her and she knew how seriously he took that oath. 'But I know nothing about your past, only that you went to boarding school. Nothing about what made you who you are.'

'What do you want to know? I promised to share.'

Yet she saw the hint of reserve in his eyes. She guessed that a long time ago, he'd retreated into himself, throwing up a defensive wall far more impenetrable than hers. He'd even hinted his early life had been difficult.

She wanted to ask about that hurt, for hurt it clearly was. She wanted to know about his strained relationship with his mother, and whether he had other family. The way he'd spat the word *socialite* more than once as if it were a curse intrigued her.

But asking him to spill his deepest secrets might push him away. He was the most self-contained person she knew. So she'd begin small.

'How do you know Dimitria Politis?'

CHAPTER ELEVEN

SURPRISE MADE FOTIS jerk his chin up. *That* was what she most wanted to know? Rosa never ceased to surprise him. He'd expected something deeply probing, or painfully personal.

Like what she'd just revealed to him.

He was surprised and, he realised, honoured that she'd shared such intimate confidences.

True, they'd been mainly about her mother rather than herself, but he knew they affected her deeply. It didn't take a genius to realise her mother's experiences had impacted on Rosa. They'd affected him.

'Dimi's a friend, that's all.'

It hit him suddenly that perhaps Rosa thought he wanted to be more than a friend to Dimi. Could she be jealous?

The thought barely lasted a second. Dimi was too young and naïve for a man like him. She couldn't hold a candle to the woman beside him, whose self-contained façade concealed a vibrant passion and a generosity he couldn't get enough of.

'Come on, Fotis. Surely you can share just a little.'

Her tone was full of tongue-in-cheek challenge yet he saw disappointment in her expression. Did she think he was reneging on their bargain?

'I can and will. In the meantime you need to eat. You didn't have breakfast.'

Since when had he worried about what a lover ate?
Since Rosa. Only Rosa.

An electric frisson of warning crept across his skin but he dismissed it. He was being considerate, that's all. He'd interrupted her meal with his questions.

He plucked an olive from the container and leaned across to pop it into her mouth. Inevitably his fingertips brushed those plump, soft lips and he had to snatch his hand back. He'd promised her words, not seduction.

'I've known Dimi since she was a baby. We don't see each other much but we're family friends.' He paused then admitted, 'That's rare for me.' Because he had no family. None that he cared to acknowledge.

Rosa didn't speak, just nodded as she covered another piece of rich, nutty bread with slices of feta and tomato.

'Her grandfather was a good friend of my father's.'

That made Rosa catch his gaze but instead of commenting she took a bite of her food and this time he watched her eyes flicker, half closed in pleasure at the flavour. She was a woman who used all her senses.

He particularly liked her fondness for tasting and touching. A tremor of carnal pleasure scudded along his spine and he made himself look away.

'Both my parents were only children.' He knew it to be true in his father's case. For his mother he only had her word for it, which proved nothing. She reinvented herself regularly to suit whatever role she wanted to play. He forged on. 'So I didn't have aunts, uncles and cousins. But Costas Politis has always been like an uncle to me. My father died when I was young and—'

'How young?'

'Five.'

Her hand closed gently around his forearm. 'I'm sorry. It must have been terrible to lose your dad when you were so young.'

Her eyes were stormy grey, sincere with regret, and he felt a strange churning in his chest. Her sympathy dredged up ancient feelings of loss and pain that he hadn't let himself dwell on for decades.

With them came half-forgotten memories.

His father's voice, deep and kind. Riding those broad shoulders down to the sea where his *Baba* taught him to float and later to fish. Lying curled up on a chair in the dappled shade of a vine-covered courtyard, listening to the murmur of male voices and the quick click-click of tavli pieces moving around a playing board. His *Baba's* patience when Fotis scrambled up onto his lap, begging to play. That was how Fotis had learned his numbers, moving counters across the inlaid board, the soft rumble of his *Baba's* voice counting with him.

'It was a long time ago.' Yet strangely his throat felt tight.

'Anyway, Costas did what he could to be a mentor, though I didn't see him often.' He read Rosa's curiosity but she didn't ask, just waited for whatever he would share. Which made him decide to share just a little more. 'I lived with my mother for a while after my father died but I was sent away to school within a year.'

Rosa's fingers dug into his arm. 'That's *very* young, especially for a boy who's lost his father.'

'It was.' It was unspeakably hard, but no worse than facing his mother's neglect. He shrugged. 'Over the years Costas stayed in contact, tried to help where he could. He stood up for my right to inherit. I've always respected him for that.'

'Sorry, I don't understand. There was some doubt over your inheritance?'

It wasn't something he spoke about but he *had* been the one to mention it. Besides, it was a matter of public record, if one had the resources to dig deep enough. His mother had done her best to bury it.

'My father was wealthy. He left my mother an annuity, but the bulk of his estate was left in trust to me. It was managed independently and my mother had no access to it.' Fotis stared at the sea and the progress of a proud, white yacht, heading for the horizon. 'She challenged the will. She wanted control of everything. If she'd succeeded there would have been nothing left for me when I came of age.'

'She'd have spent it all?' No mistaking the shock in Rosa's tone.

'She'd have squandered it as quickly as she could. My father must have known that, to make his will that way.'

It pained him to know his *Baba* must by that stage have been disillusioned about the woman he'd married.

'Costas Politis is a respected and highly successful businessman,' he explained. 'His intervention helped ensure she didn't succeed. He guarded my father's fortune and later mentored me about business. He helped me make the most of the investments I'd inherited as well as building a new, highly successful enterprise. He was my last link to my father.'

Mouth dry, Fotis swallowed a mouthful of wine and turned to his companion. 'I like the man and I'm indebted to him. He's old now and ill, so when I can I keep a friendly eye on his orphaned granddaughter. Dimi had a difficult time after her parents died. She's impulsive and insecure and—'

'The perfect target for a greedy con man. Then I broke

her heart by having a public fling with her boyfriend, even though I knew they were together. No wonder you hated me.'

'*Pretending* to have a fling,' he corrected.

She lifted her shoulders. 'The result was the same.'

'But your intentions weren't.' Their eyes locked and he felt that familiar pulse between them. Only this time the connection was far more emotional than physical. 'You saved her. Did I thank you for that?'

Rosa looked away, reaching for a slice of apricot tart. 'There's no need.'

'There's every need. You brought public speculation and censure on yourself for her sake. As random acts of kindness go, that's a big one.'

'My reputation can stand it. Besides, it was already less than pristine.'

'Because of those photos taken in your teens?'

For a second she held his gaze, then stared at the dessert in her hand as if wondering how it got there. She put it down. 'Yes.'

'Even though some of them were fake?'

Her head snapped up. 'You know about that?'

'Part of my job is sieving information for the truth.' He paused. 'I didn't pay much attention to them in the beginning but then after a while, when I knew you better, I wondered and took another look. You were the object of a concerted smear campaign.'

Rosa blinked, staring.

'You didn't know?'

Her mouth twisted. 'Oh, I knew. But no one believed me.'

'Who did you tell?' But the answer was obvious. 'Your father?'

'The first photos were real.' She shook her head. 'Why I thought it was a good idea to go to that nightclub in a minidress, when I had to climb out of a low-slung sports car...' She paused. 'The kiss was real, and yes, I'd had more alcohol than I should. But the photos made things appear far worse than what actually happened. The stories printed with them made them look like something completely different.'

Fotis remembered. The implication had been that she'd partied with her boyfriend and later had sex with him in the back of a car. It had been implied that she'd then had sexual encounters with some of his friends while drunk or high.

'The worst of the pictures were Photoshopped,' he added. 'I assume they hit the press after you broke up with your boyfriend?'

She nodded. 'He wasn't as clever as he thought. If he hadn't bragged about his influence in royal circles, I mightn't have discovered the truth until much later. A palace bureaucrat came to me, concerned about rumours that she and some others were going to lose their jobs to outsiders. She'd traced the stories to my boyfriend. When I confronted him, he blustered, but not well enough. He tried to explain with half-truths but his lies weren't good enough.

'He'd said he loved me but it was obvious he only saw me as a means to further his career and his friends'.' She drew a slow breath. 'I had him barred from the palace and never spoke to him again.'

'So he took revenge by blackening your reputation,' Fotis growled. He made a mental note to look into the guy's current situation and make life as difficult as possible for him. 'Why didn't your father help? He had the power to take some of the heat out of the stories.'

'He thought it was beneath the royal family to sue. Some of the worst photos, where they'd used my face and someone else's body, were taken down. Not that he believed they were fakes. He refused to listen. Insisted I learn the consequences of my actions and lumbered me with close personal protection for years. After that, even if I'd wanted to have a drink with friends in private, I'd never have managed it. I became a social pariah.'

Fotis' chest clamped painfully around his fast-beating heart. No wonder she'd vibrated with dislike at having another bodyguard.

Her story only made her courage in standing up for Dimi more remarkable. She'd put herself in the firing line of public censure for a stranger.

He groped for her hand and held it tight.

'You're a remarkable woman, Rosa.' Misty eyes turned to his and he wished things could have been different for her. 'I hope your father realised that eventually.'

She snorted. 'Hardly. According to him I was too like my mother. Emotional, reckless, more likely to act on the spur of the moment than follow royal protocol or common sense.'

'Your father sounds like a prig and a fool.'

She laughed, the sound snapping some of the tension that had grown as he heard her story. 'But a powerful prig.'

'And your mother... She was an incredibly popular queen.'

'Exactly. Far more popular than him. He liked everything done his way. He didn't like change or spontaneity.'

And Rosa, beneath her public veneer of calm elegance, was both spontaneous and passionate, bewitchingly so.

Fotis began to realise how tough her home life must have been, especially after her mother died.

'It seems like we were both cursed with one good parent and one we'd rather forget.'

She turned her hand to thread her fingers through his, chuckling. 'It's incredible we turned out so well adjusted, isn't it?'

Fotis' lips stretched in a rare grin. He was a recluse who specialised in keeping people at a distance. And for all Rosa's warmth, he suspected she had few true friends.

He found it hard to trust, women in particular, and he'd long ago decided not to have a family because caring deeply risked far too much pain. Nico's death still haunted him.

He suspected Rosa found it difficult to trust, men especially, and though she claimed to live her life exactly as she wanted, she felt the need to prove that to the press and the world at large. Which meant they still affected her decisions and she wasn't as free as she believed.

'You're right. We *are* incredible.'

He pressed his lips to her knuckles, hearing her indrawn breath. Her turned her hand over and tasted apricots.

His luscious woman.

She shuddered as he kissed her palm. 'Fotis.'

Her voice was a raw whisper that sent longing straight and hard to his groin.

'I want you, Rosa. Now.'

Her eyes darkened. 'Yes.'

Fotis tugged her closer, unbearably aroused by her answering desire. She never played coy games. He loved her ardour. It fed his own. Instead of dimming, their passion glowed hotter and more urgent with each day that passed. It was beyond anything he'd experienced.

But he refused to stop and analyse why.

'The food.' She was on her knees beside him, pushing aside platters.

But Fotis couldn't wait. Usually he could conjure at least a semblance of patience but something had changed as they shared their stories. Something deep and raw had opened inside him and he *needed* her *now*.

His heart ached for the pain she suffered. At the same

time he was proud of her courage, her determination to stand strong despite others' judgement.

And her tenderness... There was something addictive about her tenderness.

Impatient, he swept aside the picnic. The wine bottle fell over, dousing his ankle through his sock. He didn't even look. He only had eyes for Rosa, pulling her closer.

'Lift your leg over me,' he commanded, voice harsh.

Instead of taking issue with his tone, she favoured him with a sultry smile that undid another of the complicated, emotion-proof knots he'd tied around his heart. He *felt* it come free, but didn't worry. He'd spent so long building barriers it would take more than a smile to destroy them all.

Rosa lifted her leg over his hips as he thrust a hand in his pocket and dragged out a condom.

Her eyebrows arched as she took it from him and tore it open with her teeth. 'Boy Scout?'

'Something like that,' he muttered as he fumbled to open his jeans. Now wasn't the time to explain that from the time of his father's death he'd learned to be hyper-alert, planning ahead. He'd had to anticipate his mother's mood swings and other dangers, like the one that had taken Nico from him.

But this time even the thought of his failure to protect his little brother couldn't dim Fotis' arousal.

Finally he pulled himself free of his jeans and underwear.

'Let me.' She shuffled back, her red dress teasing his erection until she brushed the cotton aside and leaned forward to smooth on the condom.

Fotis wanted to push her hands away. He gritted his teeth and summoned all his strength not to lose himself at her deliberate, slow strokes as she smoothed the rubber down his rigid length.

But nothing in this world could have made him look away.

No woman had ever been more seductive. Her pouting concentration as she worked and the press of peaked nipples against her dress were enough to make him wonder how long he'd last.

'Rosa!' It was a growl of warning but instead of retreating, she smiled and shuffled closer, kneeling high above him.

'Fotis?'

He heard the hint of laughter, the self-congratulatory tone of a woman who knew he was at her mercy. He adored it.

With Rosa he'd discovered sex could be fun. That spending the night with a lover could be a delight, rather than the potential burden he'd believed. For she'd made it clear all she expected was a short-term relationship.

Just as well, because that was all he could give.

'Rosa,' he purred, reaching under her dress, stroking up her satiny thigh to the narrow strip of lace between her legs. It was gratifyingly wet.

She tilted her pelvis, pushing against him as he rubbed the heel of his hand against her core. She bit her bottom lip, eyelids lowering as she ground against his touch.

Her hand tightened as she tested his length, almost sending him over the edge.

He lifted his other hand to her breast, cupping it through the thin fabric. She moaned softly as he pinched her nipple and rubbed it between thumb and forefinger.

She scrabbled to lift her skirt, shifting forward until his erection nudged her underwear. Fotis dragged the lace barrier aside, felt her sink, just a centimetre till he was notched at her entrance.

'Ready?' Her wetness and the light tang of feminine arousal in the air told him she was. But he was far past the point of patient seduction and wanted her primed to accommodate him. He didn't want to hurt her.

'Ready?' She shook her head as she covered his hand with hers, pressing it hard against her breast as she circled her hips, tantalising him with the promise of what was to come. 'I've been ready since before you unzipped your jeans. What are you waiting for?'

'Well, if you're sure...' He slid his hand from beneath hers, her groan of regret turning to a sigh of anticipation as he shoved both hands under her skirt. He clamped her hips and, holding her stare, yanked her down as he thrust high off the ground.

Heaven had another name. Rosa.

Slick, tight muscles. Velvety heat that clutched at him as he pushed deep, impossibly deep, until he was embedded and there was no space between them.

Sharp pain sliced his chest as he forgot to breathe, but it was a small price to pay for the euphoria of their joining.

Her breasts rose on a jerky breath. 'Okay?' he croaked, unsure if pleasure or pain drew her features tight.

Until she nodded, gasping, 'You don't know how okay.'

She leaned forward, planting her hands on his shoulders. The changed angle slid him even further in, if that were possible. It felt so incredible, *she* felt so incredible, he couldn't trust his senses. Surely nothing had ever been this perfect?

Still gripping her hips, Fotis lifted her just a little, circling his hips, watching her expression change from taut to shocked pleasure. Again he pulled her down hard as he thrust, setting off detonations of piercing pleasure.

Their gasps mingled before being swept away in the sea breeze.

'More,' she demanded, lifting her hips.

Fotis revelled in his demanding lover, so eager for everything he could give her. Then thoughts spiralled away as he leaned up and drew her nipple into his mouth through the fine fabric and lust took over.

Jerking his hips higher, he slammed her down to meet him, senses overloading at the sheer perfection of them together. He sucked at her breast as she rotated her pelvis and threw them both off the pinnacle into bliss.

Fire engulfed him. Planets collided and splintered. Through it all he held Rosa tight, riding the shock waves, hearing her whimpers of pleasure.

Ages later when it was over, he lifted shaky hands to pull her down to collapse onto his chest. He felt her heart hammering, her breath steamy against his chest where his shirt had torn open. Her hair tickled his skin.

She was a dead weight, all that softness pressed against him. The air smelled of sex, the sea, and the cinnamon-vanilla scent of the only woman to undo him completely.

He'd never felt so...happy.

For the first time since adulthood he didn't question the rare sensation or try to analyse it. He just tightened his arms about her and let himself drift in a haze of well-being.

CHAPTER TWELVE

'WHAT WAS THE favour Leon agreed to do for you, Fotis?' Rosamund fixed her earring and looked at his reflection in the mirror of the vast en suite bathroom.

The man looked utterly scrumptious in a dark suit and crisp, white shirt. She was astounded she resisted the urge to drag him back to bed. But then, she acknowledged ruefully, her legs were still wobbly from his early afternoon lovemaking and her body felt warm and heavy from satiation. She probably didn't have the energy to tug him to bed.

Though the glint of approval in his eyes as he met her gaze made her wonder.

'He's backing a range of initiatives, including an updated international convention, to strengthen protection for children worldwide.'

'That sounds like something he'd do anyway.' She mightn't be close to Leon but he was a decent man. Anything to support vulnerable children would interest him.

Fotis nodded, his brow drawing down as he put on cufflinks. Because he was concentrating, or because of something else? He looked suddenly sombre.

'Yes, he'd always intended to sign the new convention on behalf of Cardona. But now he's also lobbying countries that are wavering about signing. Looking after children is one of those things everybody agrees on, but often their welfare ends up too low on the list of actual government priorities. It's time for that to change.'

She secured her second earring and said, 'Let me guess. They're afraid that if they sign the agreement they'll be held to account to do what they promise.'

His stern mouth rucked up at the corner and her heart gave a stupid little flutter. 'You've been around politicians too long. That's exactly it.'

'You've been working on this for some time?' She'd heard about the initiative but didn't know details. She'd look it up tonight, or perhaps tomorrow morning, since they were attending a party today.

'Years, but finally real progress is close.'

'That's wonderful.' She had some idea how long it took to finalise international initiatives. But her attention wasn't so much on the process as on Fotis and why this was important to him.

They'd spent a month on his island, an amazingly contented, wonderful month together with no sign of any threat, though the complicated fraud case against Ricardo was taking longer than expected to finalise.

Every day she woke with a feeling of well-being unlike anything she'd known. Not simply because she was safe, but because of Fotis and what they shared. Sex but friendship too, a bond she couldn't describe but which she'd miss terribly when she left.

Rosamund straightened her sapphire-blue dress. Fotis had given her glimpses into his past but she yearned to know more. She wanted to know everything about him, especially what made him determined to remain a recluse all his life.

'It's an important cause, Fotis. But I'm surprised at your

level of involvement. Is there a particular reason you're so focused on this?'

He was knotting his tie but made a hash of it, jerking it too tight so he had to tug it undone and start again. 'Isn't it enough that it's worth doing?'

The angle of his jaw and his guarded eyes made her want to step up and help him. Not because she was an expert on men's ties—she wasn't—but because some sixth sense warned he needed her.

Suddenly she sensed his disquiet. It rippled off him, an invisible force field designed to repel. She remembered it from the first days they'd known each other. Then he'd had an air of such self-containment she'd imagined nothing could breach it.

Or was she fooling herself? Fotis had always been self-possessed. Did he really *need* her?

She'd believed their intimacy was more than skin-deep but now she thought about it, *she'd* been the one to reveal so much about her past. Fotis had let her in but only a little way.

Mood dropping, she reached for her purse. For all their recent intimacy, there were still things he didn't want to share and she wasn't going to push.

'I'm ready. I'll wait in the bedroom.'

On her second step, warmth shackled her wrist. She looked down to see his hand loosely circling hers. Slowly she lifted her gaze. Blue-green eyes shimmered with a heat that scorched.

'Stay. Please.' His Adam's apple jerked as he swallowed. 'It's not something I talk about, ever.' His voice dropped to a rough-hewn, subterranean level that rumbled through her insides. 'But maybe it's time.'

Her hurt softened but she didn't want a forced confidence. 'It's okay, Fotis. I respect your need for privacy.'

The man was entitled to his secrets. Given his reaction to an innocent question, she was sure there *was* a secret behind his unwillingness to talk. Their relationship hadn't changed as much as she'd thought. Of course it hadn't.

'But I want to tell you.'

He didn't look like a man happy at the prospect, so she said nothing.

'It felt good the other day, telling you about my parents and my inheritance.' He must have noticed her eyes widen because he nodded, the lines of tension around his mouth disappearing. 'It's true. I haven't talked about that before, but it felt like a weight had lifted, sharing that.'

She stared. 'You haven't talked with *anyone*?'

He shook his head. 'Only with Costas Politis. He already knew the situation.'

Rosamund shook her head in disbelief.

But how many confidantes have you got? You've learnt to bottle up your problems too.

'I'll be ready in a second, once I get this tie right. We can talk on the way to the wedding.'

'If you like.'

'I do like.' He released her wrist, his fingers skimming up her forearm, making her shiver when they reached her inner elbow. Abruptly he dropped his hand but the expression in his eyes turned that shiver into a languid shudder of arousal. 'Have I told you you're beautiful?'

Pleased, she stroked her hand down the smooth fabric. 'Thank you. I wasn't sure what to wear to a village wedding.'

'What you're wearing is perfect. Dressy but not fussy. But I wasn't talking about the dress, I meant *you*.'

To Rosamund's surprise, she felt flustered as well as delighted. She was used to compliments, just as she was used to criticism about what she wore or how she carried herself. It came with the territory. People either flattered royals or found fault.

But this was different, not a careless compliment but meaningful.

'So are you.' There was beauty in the hard-hewn lines of his face and as for his body... Her breathing quickened.

Something flared in his eyes and he whipped around to face the mirror, concentrating on his tie. 'Maybe it's best if you wait in the bedroom. Otherwise we'll be late.'

Rosamund was still secretly smiling as they drove down the winding road in his four-wheel-drive.

'You asked why I'm interested in protecting children.' That tore her attention from the stunning view and to the man beside her, easily handling the vehicle down the narrow road. 'They bear the brunt of social problems. They're vulnerable and too often we take it for granted that their families will look after them. That's not always the case.'

'I know. Sometimes families and children struggle.' That was a factor in her own work. As well as bringing joy, she hoped her stories encouraged resilience in the children and young people who read them.

'Plus...' He paused and she deliberately turned her attention from his strong profile to the road, giving him space. 'Things happened that make me want to make changes for the better.'

He's talking about his mother, trying to steal his inheritance. What else did she do?

Rosamund suppressed a shiver. She suspected this wasn't going to be pleasant, but for his sake, and her own, she needed to hear.

'I understand that.'

After a pause he said, 'My mother was beautiful and vivacious but not maternal. I assume she had me to please my father and after he died her focus was on finding another rich man to support her. I realised much later that I cramped her style so she sent me off to boarding school. But when she sent for me again, I thought she'd changed and wanted to be with me.'

Another pause. Longer this time. 'It turned out her lover wanted kids and she wanted to prove what a doting mother she was. It was confusing. She'd never played with me or read bedtime stories before. Only my *Baba* had done that. She got angry when I asked why she'd changed.'

Rosamund couldn't help it, she reached out and touched his sleeve. 'One loving parent and one cold and distant. It sounds like my parents but in reverse. But your situation—'

'It's okay. I was safe and well fed.'

Yet her heart squeezed for the little boy confused to find himself at the centre of his mother's affection for the first time.

'Did they marry?'

'They did and I was glad. I liked my stepfather and I wasn't sent back to boarding school because he liked having me at home. Then my half-brother was born. Little Nico used to follow me around.'

'And you were a protective big brother.'

His head swung around. 'How did you know?'

'It's there in your voice.' That made her terribly sad, because she guessed this didn't have a happy ending. She knew how loyal Fotis was to his father's friend, Costas, and the man's granddaughter. She couldn't imagine Fotis being so isolated now if his brother were around.

'He was a good kid.' Fotis steered them around a curve. 'But my mother didn't have luck with her husbands. Mine died in an accident and Nico's was diagnosed with aggressive leukaemia when he was still young. She was widowed again, but that time she had more money to enjoy herself. She packed us both off overseas to boarding school.'

Rosamund cleared her tight throat. Now she understood his coldness when speaking of his mother.

'Nico was a quiet kid and little. He got bullied. I was continually in trouble, fighting the bullies. It didn't help that Nico didn't speak English, plus I stood out because of my maths skills. Being called a prodigy didn't make me many friends. It didn't endear me to the maths master either. He seemed to take it as a personal affront, always looking at ways to take me down a peg or two.'

'What happened?'

Fotis' hands tightened on the wheel. 'The older boys waited until I was away from the school at a chess tournament, then locked Nico in an unused cupboard next to the maths classroom. He was there for hours. When the door was finally unlocked he was unconscious. He was asthmatic and would have been terrified.' Fotis' voice had a steely ring. 'He died.'

'I—' Words failed her. 'That's appalling.'

'Children need protecting, even ones in expensive schools.' He expelled a slow breath as if searching for control. 'It needn't have happened. One of the students overheard what the other boys had done and told the maths master since he was nearest. The master told him to mind his own business, that a little interaction with the older boys would toughen Nico's character.'

'Fotis!'

He pulled over to the side of the road and switched off the engine. 'The man was sacked. Eventually. At first they didn't want to believe the boy. Until others came forward with stories of bullying. There was quite a scandal though a lot was hushed up.'

She reached for his hand and held it in both of hers. 'And you? It must have been...' She shook her head. 'I can't imagine.'

One callused finger brushed her cheek with a gentleness that defied the harsh set of his jaw. 'I survived. I grew tough. I got into a lot of trouble as a teen but Costas Politis helped me, made sure I didn't go off the rails completely. Then I went into the army. The discipline changed my life, and then I found a chance to use my skills. Ah, Rosa, don't.'

She bit her trembling lip and nodded. She wasn't a teary person but his story, his and Nico's, broke her heart.

'Don't worry about me! I'm fine.'

She waved away his concern, embarrassed by it when *he* was the one who'd suffered. But that concern warmed her too. He *cared* about her. His tenderness made something inside her grow and blossom. A warmth she had no name for.

So much made sense now. His contempt for his mother. His dour determination to remain a loner. She knew he still felt his brother's loss deeply. Then there were his strong protective instincts. Even when he'd despised her he'd done everything necessary to keep her safe.

Despite his stern air and his determination to cut himself off, that protectiveness was intrinsic in him.

She'd never felt safer with anyone in her life. But she felt so much more too.

Maybe that explained the strange, fluttery feeling in her chest as he closed the space between them.

'It's okay, Rosa. It was long ago.' His gaze pinioned hers. 'The past makes us what we are but we keep going, don't we? We have that in common. The past has made us stronger.'

It was one of the most affirming things anyone had ever said to her. The most surprising.

She'd spent her adult life reminding herself she was strong, that she'd moved on past hurts and errors. That she could face anything. But no one had acknowledged that in her. Sometimes, on her down days, it was hard to feel so certain about herself.

Fotis' words made her feel strong, as if she could face anything, yet simultaneously left her craving more, craving things she'd told herself weren't for her. Emotional attachment. Belonging.

His warm hand cupped the back of her neck and he pulled her towards him, his mouth brushing hers as lightly as a morning breeze drifting across her skin.

Instantly she opened for him, breathing in his scent, his taste, her hands clinging to his straight shoulders. He was so solid, so imposing, yet his kiss was heartbreakingly gentle.

Did he know how that tenderness undid her? How precious it was?

No one had ever kissed like this.

As if he wanted to make her whole. As if she meant everything to him.

The shocking thought speared her consciousness. But then he stroked her lips with his tongue, pausing as if seeking permission before delving deeper, and thoughts splintered.

She clung to him, trembling at the vast, burgeoning emotion that spread and spread until it filled her up.

'Fotis. Please, I...'

'*Asteri mou.*'

The words feathered her mouth and she knew what they meant now. My star. She'd looked them up.

She'd told herself it was a random endearment delivered in the throes of passion. But they weren't having sex now.

Those two little words felt powerful. As if signifying something monumental.

Rosamund pulled back a little, needing to read his expression. But her withdrawal shattered the moment. She saw his unfocused gaze sharpen and he muttered something in Greek. 'The wedding. We're going to be late if we don't move now.'

Dazed, she nodded, hearing the words and knowing he was right, yet unable to move away.

Fotis caught her hand and pressed it to his mouth, his kiss to her palm a promise for later. She had to be content with that. She couldn't be utterly selfish and keep him from the wedding. These were his friends and she suspected he didn't have many true friends.

Scrounging up a semblance of determination, she sat back in her seat. 'Later,' she whispered.

His mouth unfurled in a slow smile that heated her to the core and spoke of pleasures to come. 'Absolutely.'

Then he turned and switched on the engine.

Rosamund couldn't remember the last time she'd enjoyed herself so much. The whole village had gathered under the plane trees in the square after the wedding ceremony.

The whitewashed church had been small and there'd been standing room only. Dark icons in polished metal frames decorated the walls. The scent of incense filled the space. So did the gravity of the couple's vows, even though Rosamund didn't understand a word, and the sheer joy of the occasion.

She still felt unsettled by the unexpectedly intense emotions she'd experienced, witnessing the wedding. It felt more real somehow, more meaningful, than any she'd attended.

Now, she was surrounded by people of all ages gathered around tables that had been brought out of houses and placed together so the community could celebrate as one. Snowy cloths covered the tables, some of them beautifully embroidered in what looked like traditional designs. Platters of food were emptying but the delicious scent of grilled food wafted from where a group of men manned a huge charcoal barbecue.

'More wine?' Fotis held the unlabelled bottle above her small glass tumbler.

No elegant stemware here, no silver service. Yet it was the most wonderful meal she'd ever eaten. Delicious and authentic in a way all those gourmet meals at exclusive events could never match. Perhaps because the people here were warm and genuine and she'd never felt so at home.

'*Ne, epharisto.*'

Irini, sitting across the table from her, grinned. 'Bravo!' She turned to the woman next to her, one of the bride's cousins. 'Our visitor speaks Greek.'

Immediately several people down the table clamoured for more information and the old lady switched to Greek, speaking emphatically and at far more length than Rosamund's couple of words warranted.

'I only said *yes, thanks*,' Rosamund whispered to Fotis as he poured her wine.

'Ah.' There was a twinkle in his eyes that she'd begun to see occasionally. She adored it. 'But your pronunciation was perfect and everyone has noticed how much you're improving. Now several people are claiming credit for your language skills.'

Rosamund leaned in, revelling in his closeness. 'Every time I come to the village someone teaches me a new phrase.'

He put the bottle down. 'You've impressed them. It's a compliment that you've begun using Greek phrases. Not every visitor bothers to learn any, and given most of the people here understand English it's not absolutely necessary.'

Before she could respond a hand reached for her. It was the bride, wearing a beaming smile. Around the square women were rising from their seats, joining hands to form a line as the musicians struck up a new tune.

Rosamund had done her share of dancing, from waltzing under chandeliers at royal balls to following the beat in the loud, thrumming heat at nightclubs. She'd never danced in the dappled shade of a cobblestoned square. Or with Fotis' eyes on her.

The dance was beautiful and deeply moving. Perhaps because of the group's bonhomie and their encouragement as she stumbled through the steps until eventually she learned the rhythm, as if she really were one of them. Or maybe it was because of the way the bride glowed with happiness. Or the expression on the face of her new husband, Fotis' friend and colleague, Tassos. He watched his bride as if he could never get his fill of her.

That only made Rosamund keenly aware of Fotis' gaze on her. She didn't meet his stare but *felt* it in every pore. Felt the thrum of awareness, the knowing, the anticipation, and something deeper too.

Then it was time for the men to dance. Tassos, shaking his head and pointing to his prosthetic leg, swooped his wife into his arms and onto his lap as he sat down at the table. Rosamund watched with interest as he said something to Fotis who, after what looked like initial refusal, stood, stripped off his jacket and rolled up his sleeves. He'd already discarded his tie.

The music was different this time, slow but with an energy that built and built. Again the dancers formed a line with first one then another taking the lead and adding embellishments to the regular steps. There were stately older men, surprisingly light on their feet, and young would-be acrobats who garnered whoops of approval.

Then Fotis took the lead, his expression grave and his steps measured, until suddenly he sprang high, his hand connecting with his outstretched leg, before dropping low in a manoeuvre that required incredible athleticism. His movements were precisely controlled, with sudden bursts of energy as he spun, rose and dropped only to rise again with an ease that astonished her.

Together the rhythm of the music, the steady clapping, and the raw emotion harnessed in his movements, stole her breath. She was on the edge of her seat, wondering at the pounding of her heart. Then someone else took the lead and Fotis moved back to give them space.

His gaze locked on hers, bright and searching, and the music faded, obliterated by the roar of white noise in her ears.

It felt like they were alone, despite the crowd, the claps and cheers. Fotis looked at her and it seemed the most natural thing in the world for her heart to rise against her ribs, its beat quickening at her instant, all-consuming awareness.

Awareness and acceptance. Acceptance at the joy she felt. At the knowledge this man and no other had forged such an intimate connection with her. That this was the man, would always be the man, she wanted by her side.

Her breath hitched as her brain caught up with her heart. It should be impossible, given her history with the opposite sex. Given the difficulty she had building trust in anyone.

Yet instead it was perfectly easy.

She was in love, utterly, wholeheartedly in love with Fotis Mavridis.

CHAPTER THIRTEEN

THE DAY AFTER the wedding, everything felt different.

They'd both enjoyed the wedding. Fotis had been surprised how much, since his natural inclination was to refuse group celebrations. But Tassos was his closest friend, one of a very few. In the end it had been easy and fun.

Rosa had made it fun, drawing him in so he forgot the reasons he usually avoided such events.

He didn't even mind that he'd opened up about his past. Remarkably, even knowing his secrets were no longer completely secret didn't bother him. He knew she'd respect his privacy.

Later, in bed… The sex only got better. Even the aftermath, lying with her in his arms, felt like nothing he'd known. Almost frighteningly good.

He frowned as he exited the house and made for the old orchard where she'd been for the last half hour.

Frighteningly good.

Why be frightened? Their time together was an unexpected gift. Spectacular sex. A sense of well-being more satisfying than any time he could recall. Engaging conversations that often challenged and stretched him. The best sleep he could remember.

Frightening because it's all about to end. Because you don't want it to be over. You like her too much.

He tried to dismiss the idea but a creeping feeling of dismay tightened his nape, confirming it.

The phone call he'd just received changed everything. But he realised, everything had already begun to change. Now the lingering glow inside conflicted with a new, jittery feeling in the pit of his stomach. Regret.

He wasn't ready for this liaison to end. But of course it must. They'd both known it from the start, and it had lasted longer than either had anticipated.

For the first time in many years however, logic was no match for his feelings.

That's what should frighten you. Feelings. For Rosa.

Fotis paused in the arched entrance to the orchard, his hand on the old stonework for support. He needed it as he grappled with his emotions.

Rosa sat on a chair in the dappled shade. Her head was bent over her journal, pencil racing across the page. Her strawberry-blond hair gleamed where the sun caught it, amber and gold. In cut-off shorts and a T-shirt, with a haphazard bun and her sandals kicked off, one foot tucked beneath her, she stole his breath.

There was no artifice about her. She was simply Rosa and he needed—

His hands clenched.

Not *needed. Desired. There's a difference.*

He'd designed his life around the absolute requirement that he be separate. Independent. Alone. He didn't *need* anyone.

The grief he felt over his brother's death, and the guilt—because he knew Nico wouldn't have been targeted if not for him—were permanently branded on his soul. He should have been there to protect his little brother. He'd failed him and nothing, ever, could change that.

The early loss of his father, then his stepfather, and his mother's narcissism, reinforced his compulsion to hold himself apart because loss was a terrible void that threatened to suck the heart from a man.

Trust was tough though not, he realised now, completely impossible. He trusted Rosa. But grief and unending guilt were constant. He knew them well. He couldn't, wouldn't, make himself vulnerable again.

He'd let her under his guard and it had felt like the best thing he'd ever experienced. Now he saw how perilous it was, awaking yearnings for a life for which he simply wasn't cut out.

The phone call from America had come at an opportune time, before he fell heedlessly into a catastrophic error of judgement.

That didn't stop stark grief curdling his stomach. Because this was over and he didn't want it to be.

His avid gaze traced Rosa's profile. Lingered on the curve of her ear, the arch of her brow and the tiny hint of a dimple lurking at the corner of her mouth. Her resolute chin. Her nose with that tiny hint of a bump near the bridge.

The way her teeth sank into her bottom lip as she flipped to a new page and quickly started to sketch instead of write. He couldn't make out what she drew but her bold, sure strokes spoke of long practice. She was totally absorbed and he drank her in, knowing the news he brought would end this idyll.

There'd be no more moments like this.

That was good in the long term, but right now he battled an absurd, juvenile urge to forget the outside world and the harsh realities of life and pretend he hadn't taken the call.

To continue, just a little longer, as they'd been doing for... five weeks! Was it really so long?

Hauling in a deep breath scented with sunshine and growing things, he moved closer. She was so absorbed she didn't notice his approach as he came up beside her.

Angling his head he saw the image she sketched.

Pride jabbed him at her obvious talent. That was swiftly followed by astonishment, first at the subject, then at some unexpectedly familiar details. The angled eyebrows he saw in the mirror every day. They were so distinctive he'd been teased about them as a kid. The severe expression in those narrowed eyes that he'd also seen in the mirror when something annoyed him.

'So that's how you see me, is it?'

She looked up, startled. After a moment those delectable grooves appeared in her cheek as she smiled. 'I think you make a fine dragon. Don't you?'

Fotis shifted closer, his hand settling on her shoulder, needing to touch her. Not merely because the news he brought meant the end of what they shared. But because, how could he not? It was as natural as breathing for them to touch. He held back a sigh of relief as his fingers covered her bare skin and the urgent thrum of his pulse slowed just a little.

Besides, he knew how significant this moment was. Rosa's smile and her invitation to look were unprecedented. She'd never mentioned what it was she wrote in her notebook and he hadn't asked. Nor had she explained the hours she spent on the computer, though he'd guessed it was some sort of work.

He knew it was important to her. She'd spend hours at a time utterly focused. In the first weeks she'd snap shut her notebook or laptop as soon as he appeared. Lately that had changed, and he'd hoped she'd let him into her secret.

How ironic that today, probably their last day together, was the day.

Heat closed around his throat, like a massive hand squeezing the air out. Panic scrabbled at him until, with a mighty effort, he swallowed and breathed again.

Fotis studied the image, noting how the angle of the beast's impressive, raised wings mirrored the set of its eyebrows. How the image seemed alive with energy.

'It's good. It looks like it could fly off the page. But do dragons have eyebrows?'

'This one does. He draws them down when he's grumpy. Or waggles them when he laughs.'

'He laughs, then?' Stupid to feel relieved.

'Oh, yes. But only with people he trusts. At first he's all fire and brimstone. But when you get to know him he's unexpectedly charming.'

Her gaze was warm and he wanted to stay in this moment, having her look at him that way. He dragged the other ancient chair across and sat down so close their arms brushed.

The news from New York could wait. Selfishly, Fotis wanted to extend time before the real world intervened.

Coward.

He ignored the inner jibe. They couldn't have a future but he'd have this. He knew how much it meant for Rosa to open up about what she'd hidden so assiduously. It would take a worse man than he to rob her of this moment.

Besides, he wanted to know. And he was desperate to stave off what must come.

'Tell me,' he urged.

She did, slowly at first but with an enthusiasm that made her glow. How she'd always scribbled stories and drawn. Her mother had encouraged it and her father had declared it a waste of time and effort. Over time, after Rosa lost her mother and the world grew more censorious, she'd found increasing solace in writing fiction and drawing the worlds she created. It was her escape.

'It's a fantasy, part of a series for younger readers,' she explained. 'It's named after Princess Lily but my favourite is her friend, Daisy, the innkeeper's daughter. She lives in the village below the castle. She's practical and clever and competent. Lily always seems to find trouble but together they find their way out again.'

He was intrigued, not just by her words but by the images she showed him. 'And the dragon?'

'He's a newcomer and Lily's terrified of him, especially when she meets the handsome, golden-haired prince who's hunting him. He tells her terrible stories about the dragon. Until Daisy discovers the dragon's in pain, wounded by the prince's arrow. The handsome prince is a thief, trying to find the dragon's lair to search for dragon eggs and treasure. The dragon has led him away.'

Fotis huffed a laugh. 'So the grouchy dragon is a good guy, protecting his family?'

She shrugged. 'Partly. But he's not a villain. One of the themes is about not judging too quickly, not accepting at face value what someone says.'

Because handsome, plausible people weren't always who they seemed, and even grumpy beasts might prove to have hidden depths. Something swooped low from his chest to his gut.

'It's much more complicated than that and it's an adventure rather than a morality tale.' She shot him a sideways look. 'I hope you don't mind that I stole your eyebrows. And your death stare.'

That was what she called it? Was it any wonder he liked her so much?

'Fotis?' She looked suddenly unsure.

'Of course I don't mind. I feel honoured to help you visualise your dragon.' A wounded dragon. It wasn't far off the mark. For all his armour, he felt pain, knowing what was to come. 'I hope you're going to approach a publisher.'

It sounded like an intriguing story, plus it didn't hurt to learn young some of life's more painful truths. That good looks weren't always matched by a good heart. He thought of his beautiful mother and the handsome man who'd seduced and tried to use Rosa, then wrought his revenge when she rejected him.

'I already have a publisher. And readers. I have a deadline for this story.'

So his suspicions were true. Not that he'd known she wrote fiction, but he'd long since guessed Rosa did more than lead a life of leisure with a few royal engagements thrown in. 'Why haven't I heard of the books?' His search had found no mention of her writing.

She closed her notebook. 'I write under another name.'

Fotis thought it through. She'd been castigated by her father and the press for her actions and things she hadn't done. She still carried baggage from the experience.

Had she thought the critics would take their knives to her work because of who she was? Melancholy filled him at the idea of her hiding her talent.

'Why not reveal your identity to your readers? Take a bow for your own work.'

'I don't think that's a good idea.'

'Surely it's part of who you are. Even from that short description I can tell this means a lot to you. And I've seen you with young people in Paris. You connect with them and they listen to you. Not because you're royal but because you're interested and engaging.'

'I could say the same about you, playing basketball with those teens.'

They weren't talking about him. 'Don't you think your mother would have been proud, having another creative person in the family?'

Instead of answering she bent abruptly, reaching for her phone, frowning. 'I've got it on vibrate while I work, but this is the fourth time someone's tried to reach me.' She checked the number. 'It's Leon.'

'Rosa, leave it for now.'

He was too late. She'd already taken the call. He watched her hair ruffle in the breeze and couldn't help but stroke its gilded softness, astounded all over again at the instant well-being he felt with the physical connection.

Finally she hung up. 'Leon had news. But you already knew?'

He inclined his head. 'I came to tell you.'

She didn't say anything, probably wondering why he hadn't immediately told her that Ricardo was in prison and looked set to stay there a long time.

Her expression was inscrutable. 'So it's over. I don't need protection anymore.'

'Yes, it's over.'

She stared back as if waiting for more. But what could he say? Eventually she said, 'Thank you, Fotis, for looking after me. For everything.'

'It was my pleasure, you know that.'

How trite that sounded. As if protecting her had been anything other than a compulsion. He'd have done whatever it took to keep her safe.

'You'll want to return to Cardona. I'll organise—'

'There's no rush.' She looked at her hands then up at him. 'I can work here. I could stay on.'

Another man would say yes. A man who could give her more.

But Fotis knew his limits. He'd already pushed beyond them, dangerously far. He wanted Rosa to have everything she deserved, everything she desired, and suddenly he knew, from the hope in her eyes and the tension in her body, that she wanted more than a fling.

Even then, he knew a moment's weakness. It would be easy to let her stay, enjoy what they shared a little longer. But that would make parting more difficult.

'If that's what you'd like, you're most welcome. But,' he cleared his throat, 'I'm needed in Athens. Some important projects I need to oversee.'

There were always important projects and he'd set up his business so that he could work where it suited him most of the time. But she didn't need to know that.

She folded a page of her notebook, fingers working busily. 'You're going to Athens?'

He looked away, to the coast and the village where only yesterday he'd experienced such joy. Iron bands wrapped his chest, constricting his lungs, hampering his breathing.

'Initially. Then the USA and Asia.' The trip wasn't strictly necessary. But he needed to put distance between them. 'I'll be travelling for a while.'

'You're eager to get rid of me?'

The hurt in her voice brought instant denial to his lips, but he kept it in. 'Not eager, Princess. But our time's up. We have to return to our real lives.'

Fotis sensed her dismay but, true to type, only her agitated hands and rapid pulse betrayed her. And that invisible connection between them. He *felt* her shock, her hurt.

'You haven't called me Princess in over a month.'

He shrugged, ignoring the pain shrieking through taut muscles. 'If the shoe fits.'

'What if I said I don't want to go? I want to stay with you.'

'That's not possible.'

'It's not impossible, it's a choice. Yours and mine. You're saying you don't want me with you? What we share means nothing to you?'

'What we shared was beautiful.' He locked his jaw for a second, needing to ensure she couldn't read his inner struggle. 'Now it's over. It's time to return to our own lives.'

Her gaze held his and despite everything, he didn't want to look away. He was in so deep the prospect of separating hurt. Which reinforced the necessity to end this immediately.

Her soft hand covered his, stroking the ball of his thumb. 'I disagree. I want to stay with you. I love you, Fotis.'

CHAPTER FOURTEEN

IN ROMANTIC STORIES *I love you* was the catalyst for an answering declaration of love. The cue for a happy ending.

Good thing you're not really a romantic, isn't it?

Because instead Fotis stared, his mouth dropping open, before he shot to his feet and stalked away. Any faint hope that her announcement would prompt a similar one from him died.

He spun around, scowling down at her, that furrowed brow a perfect match for the dragon she'd drawn. Yet he didn't look angry so much as perplexed. Stunned.

'You really didn't know?'

She wanted to stand and face him as an equal but her legs were wobbly, so she was stuck here, staring up at him.

Just as well. If you were on your feet you'd reach for him.

Would he feel that spark of passion ignite now? Rosamund had always believed it was something they shared equally. But could it be one-sided, like her feelings?

'It's not love, Rosa. It's sex. And liking. You've been through a stressful time. Your emotions are—'

'Don't try to tell me what I'm feeling, Fotis.'

She loved him but he tried her patience. Was he wilfully blind? Did he *really* not feel this?

She forced her breathing to slow. 'I mean what I say. I'm

not prone to romantic dreams. Remember, I grew up knowing the reality behind the fairy-tale fantasy. Then my teenage love affair cured me of such yearnings.'

Or so she'd believed.

Rosamund read the sharp planes of his face—they looked harsher than usual—and felt herself melt. Even angry with him, she didn't want him hurting. She stifled a desperate sob at the inanity of that. *She* was the one in mortal pain.

'I didn't mean to fall in love with you, but I have. It's real, what I feel for you.'

He raised his hand to stop her words. 'But I told you. I made it clear that I don't do long-term relationships. I can't.'

'You did make it clear and I agreed because that was all I expected. I wasn't looking for love.' Her voice cracked. 'I thought that was for other people, not me.'

She'd never said it before, even to herself, but she'd felt she didn't deserve love. It was only with Fotis that she'd realised, despite her outward confidence, at heart she'd never felt good enough.

That was part of the reason she loved him. He'd made her feel strong and confident as no one had since her mother. He'd challenged her, fought with her, then cared for and supported her. He didn't belittle, he expected her to shine. He raised her up until she felt she *could* take on the world as she'd always told herself. Look how he'd just engaged with her about her work. He'd encouraged her, yet all the time…

Her throat jammed as pain overtook her. Finally she found the strength to surge from her seat.

Instead of closing the gap, she planted her feet, grounding herself as waves of anguish battered her.

'Emotions can't be controlled by rules, Fotis. My feelings for you sneaked up before I realised what was happening. I didn't *intend* to love you, but I do.'

He shook his head. 'I'm sorry, but—'

'I'd love you even if we couldn't have sex again, though that would be tragic. I love the person you are. Complicated and intriguing. I love your loyalty. When you give your word, you mean it. I love your kindness and your drive. That sneaky sense of humour I didn't think existed at first. I even love it when you go haughty as if your way is the only way, because I know that underneath—'

'Enough!' he barked, stepping back as if repelled.

That stole the air from her lungs. Rosamund stood tall but inside she felt herself shrivel. It had been an incredible risk, admitting her feelings, but being with Fotis had made her courageous, willing to put her pride on the line and more importantly, her heart.

Now her certainty faded. Not about her own feelings, they were immutable, but about his. How had she been so wrong? She'd looked into his eyes, felt his tenderness, and believed he felt the same.

He looked at her, aghast, as if she'd turned into a stranger. 'I'm sorry, sorrier than I say. But I don't feel the same.'

'Because you won't let yourself?' She angled her chin. 'Or do you really feel nothing for me?'

He scrubbed his hand around his neck, his scowl deepening. 'I didn't say that. I'm not a robot. Of course I feel. I like you, Rosa. I admire you and I'm deeply attracted, you know that.'

'But not enough.' Her voice was flat. He *liked* her.

She'd thought she understood him. This had begun as an affair but over time it had grown into so much more. She'd been *sure* his emotions were engaged too. Perhaps it wasn't love for him but, she'd believed, it had become something strong and undeniable.

Maybe he had a voracious sexual appetite, lots of lovers, and he made them all feel…special.

She pressed a palm to her stomach as nausea welled.

'I don't want to hurt you, Rosa.'

Her gesture cut off his words. He hadn't hurt her. She'd hurt herself, she realised abruptly.

What was it with her and self-sabotage? In her teens she'd fallen for a charming guy who wanted to get into her pants because it was a way into the royal family. Now she'd fallen for someone incapable of loving her.

Even so, she had to be absolutely, completely sure. 'I see us together, Fotis, helping each other through the tough times and celebrating the good ones.' In her mind she'd imagined lots of good times, lots of celebrations. 'Building our lives together.'

But his closed expression confirmed her worst fears. 'Weren't you listening when I talked about my past? There are reasons I'm a solitary person. I need to be alone.'

Except for occasional sex.

All this time she'd imagined a growing bond but all he felt was the pressure to satisfy his libido. To be fair, she'd accepted those terms but then everything had transformed, for her at least.

Rosamund sucked in a shuddery breath and turned to the view, past the sun-baked plain to the village and glittering sea beyond. Above hung the vast blue sky, a reminder that she was merely a tiny speck on an immense globe.

She didn't need the reminder. She felt herself shrinking, becoming smaller and smaller, wishing she could disappear.

Of course she knew about Fotis' past. But, dazzled by her feelings, she'd managed to shuck off a lifetime's insecurity and think she could help him move on. That they'd have each other's backs so together they could cast away the shadows of the past.

That *she'd* be enough for him as he was enough for her.

What were you thinking, girl?

The contemptuous voice was her father's, the sneer as vivid as if he stood there, glowering at her.

Her life had been a series of lessons in not being good enough. She'd never been able to satisfy her father's high standards. As for having a man *love* her...

Fotis said something, his voice low, but she didn't hear it over the rush of blood in her ears. She folded her arms tight around her body, failing to hold in the pain.

She wouldn't have thought it possible but she felt worse than she ever had. Worse than her father had ever made her feel, or her first, deceitful lover. Worse than when the press portrayed her in the worst possible light. She felt as bad as when she'd lost her mother.

Because no one could inflict hurt as severe as someone you loved.

That's why Fotis doesn't want a relationship. He doesn't want that pain.

She understood, but he had no right to make her feel like this. And yet she loved him. Loved, and at this moment almost hated him.

Rosamund turned, surprised to find him so close, hands dropping to his sides as if he'd been reaching for her.

Even now her imagination tried to paint the picture she wanted instead of facing the truth.

'I had you wrong.' Pain prompted the words. 'If someone asked me for a word to describe you, I'd have said strong. But you're not, are you? You're a coward. You want to stay in your eyrie, cut off from people because you're scared of loving. Do you think your father and brother would have wanted that?'

His head rocked back as if from a slap. He looked dazed, then his eyes narrowed to slits of blistering fire and his nostrils flared. 'Don't bring my family into this!'

'I—'

'Don't talk to me about fear and hiding. You're proud of living the life you say you want, but are you *really* doing that?' His voice was unrelenting. 'That last day in France we went out to lunch so you could show the world you were unfazed by the attack, enjoying yourself with your boyfriend at your side. You were so concerned about projecting an image you didn't even give yourself time to recover from the shock of the attack. Time you needed. You're not in control, you're running scared.'

His expression softened to something that looked almost like pity. Her stomach spasmed. She didn't want his pity.

'*You're* hiding, Rosa. Letting your dead father and the press dictate how you live. You worry about the image you project instead of living your life. You'd rather let the world think you're a dilettante, living off the royal purse, than tell people about your work.' He paused. 'But you're strong, when you choose to be. You don't need me to lean on.'

For the longest time she was incapable of speaking.

Never, in her wildest dreams, could she have believed today would see them hurting each other like this, ripping away protective layers and inflicting such pain.

She shoved her hands into her pockets where he couldn't see them shake. 'Don't worry, Fotis. That's one lesson I learned a long time ago. I don't need a man to lean on.'

Couldn't he see this wasn't about propping herself up but about wanting to share and build together?

'I don't *need* a man at all.' Particularly one who didn't

want her. She wanted to say it had been a mistake, she didn't love him, but couldn't do it. Her unrequited feelings were too deep to pretend.

She shoved her feet into her discarded sandals, gathering up her gear. But even with her heart crumbling, she couldn't leave him like this.

'Take a hard look at your own life, Fotis. You're not responsible for your brother's death. It wasn't your fault. As for believing you can only survive as a recluse...'

She gestured towards the village. 'You're not alone. You've been forging connections, real connections with other people. Dimitria Politis and her grandfather. Tassos and his wife think the world of you. So do the other villagers.'

Before he could interrupt she continued. 'Not because you've spent money improving the island's infrastructure. I heard them talk about you.' Everyone had anecdotes about his quiet acts of kindness, how he got things done, how he listened. Even rare examples of his dry sense of humour. 'They respect the way you roll up your sleeves and help work. They *like* you. You're not alone, Fotis, whatever you tell yourself. You've got people you care about and who care about you. That makes you stronger, not weaker.'

'Rosa...' His voice was rough with warning.

She met those ocean-coloured eyes and knew they'd haunt her dreams. Stark emotion welled and she felt that telltale prickle behind her eyes. She'd never see him again.

'Goodbye, Fotis.' She spun away. 'I'll arrange my own transport.'

'Rosa!'

She kept walking. There was only so much a woman could take. She'd reached her limit.

CHAPTER FIFTEEN

FOTIS' STRIDE SLOWED as he negotiated the throng. He'd known this renowned European book fair attracted crowds, but the vast complex teemed.

Impatience rode him, adding to the potent mix of anticipation and fear churning inside.

In the ten days since Rosa had left, his life had turned on its head. He'd let deadlines slide or alternatively micromanaged projects to the extent that he'd almost lost one of his best staff, unable to work with his suddenly interfering ways.

Fotis couldn't get the balance right. He'd thrown himself into work because for years that had been his prime focus. Since Rosa's departure it filled the empty hours. That and long workouts.

But nothing worked. He was strung out, jittery and operating on too little sleep.

He couldn't banish the memory of Rosa's dazed eyes when he rejected her. Or her gallant courage when she confronted him, forcing him to hear things he didn't want to hear, even as he read the hurt she tried to conceal. He'd never felt so emotionally stripped bare.

She loved you and you pushed her away.

He'd told himself it was the right thing. He couldn't give

her what she craved. He couldn't be the man she wanted. He hadn't dared hope she was right and he could reach out and grasp the sort of happiness she promised.

Was he a coward?

He'd rejected her words the instant she said them. Because he always faced the truth about himself. He knew he had feet of clay. He'd failed his brother. In the past he'd picked himself up and kept going, even when it felt like he'd lost everything.

But as time went on her words had gouged deeper, eating through his certainties, leaving him in darkness.

Until yesterday when he'd heard she was appearing at the book fair. Not in her royal capacity but as the author of the Princess Lily books. The surprise announcement of her identity had taken the world by storm.

He'd been stunned when he'd looked them up the night she'd left. They were a worldwide phenomenon, translated across the globe.

A unique talent...wonderful world-building...engaging and utterly authentic...a humorous but honest voice for today's young readers.

He'd burned with pride at the praise. Her stories blended a lush fairy-tale world with a relevance to today's society that hooked children and adults. Her fans had gone wild when her identity was announced.

Fotis was sorry he hadn't been with her to tell her how proud he was, of her work and of claiming her place as the author of the much-loved books.

But she wouldn't want to hear from him. What right had he to offer praise after what he'd done?

Yet circumstances had altered when he'd learned she was appearing here. He'd contacted Leon, ostensibly to discuss progress in their lobbying, but Leon had seen through that ruse. He'd complained his sister had accepted the barest minimum security arrangements for her appearances. He'd also tried to quiz Fotis about their time together.

Fotis shouldered his way through the throng, quickening his step. He'd brought in top security staff to blend in with the crowd but wouldn't be happy until he saw she was safe. Ricardo might be locked up but there were some dangerous people out there.

He slammed to a stop as he rounded a corner and saw her at a desk, dwarfed by the queue of people waiting have books signed. Others clustered, taking photos. Behind her two images filled the wall, a book cover and a photo of her, light dancing in her eyes.

Air backed up in his lungs as the noise faded. It was like the first time he'd seen her. That moment of absolute shock because he recognised this woman at a cellular level, knew her in the way of a man recognising his mate, though he hadn't realised it then.

The longing was just as fierce now, worse, because he knew he'd destroyed his chance with her.

Forcing himself to breathe, he moved in.

Rosa's hair was loose around her shoulders, its glow drawing him like a beacon. He hated that her face was pale against her cornflower-blue jacket, though her smile was bright as she chatted to a pair of teenagers.

She'd always been good at putting on a public face. Was she doing it now? Or had the thrill of connecting with her readers pushed aside the pain he'd inflicted?

Maybe she's already moved on.

Maybe she realised it wasn't love. Perhaps she's relieved to have left. She's embracing a new life that doesn't include you.

You're in her past, Mavridis. She won't thank you for pushing into her life now.

He noticed the woman standing between Rosa and the queue. His breathing eased. He'd employed the woman, hoping Rosa would be more comfortable with her than a man whose presence screamed *bodyguard*. Scanning the area, he saw other guards, incognito. At least she had some protection.

The teenagers moved on. Rosa flexed her fingers as if they were stiff and suddenly her gaze met his.

Everything in him stopped. Her eyes widened, the corners of her mouth lifting. Her smile speared him. He felt blood flow from the wound as his breathing and pulse kicked in again.

Then her half-formed smile died. She looked away, mouth firming. The woman beside her said something and Rosa turned to the next person in line.

Fotis was gutted. She'd wanted to see him. Until she remembered what he'd done.

Still, he wasn't going anywhere. Not until he'd spoken with her. That was non-negotiable.

For the next couple of hours he watched, feeling the too-heavy thud of his bruised heart against his ribs. In all that time she didn't look his way.

That tells you all you need to know.

Yet he stood his ground, until finally staff erected a sign stating that the signing had ended for the day, setting up a cordon.

Fotis moved in, nodding to the security staff. Rosa was talking to a woman he recognised as her agent. They were at the rear of the space, backs to him, yet Rosa sensed him approach. Her shoulders rose, spine stiffening. She turned.

'I'm afraid the signing's over,' the other woman said. 'You can come back tomorrow.'

'Rosa?' Still she said nothing. This close, he read her fatigue. Despite the smile she'd worn for the crowd, her eyes were dull. Exhaustion from the signing or something else?

Beads of sweat prickled his nape as he moved nearer and the agent stepped in front of him.

'It's okay, Carlotta. I know him. I'll join you soon.'

You don't even deserve an introduction. Do you really think she'll listen?

Fotis ignored the voice, shoving his hands deep in his trouser pockets. Because it took everything he had not to reach for Rosa, wrap his arms around her and pull her in tight.

Rosamund had plumbed the depths of despair since leaving Greece, telling herself things would get better as she moved on with her life. Now she learnt she'd been wrong. The anguish of seeing him again, realising separation hadn't diminished her feelings, almost tore her apart.

His severe features had never been more starkly compelling. It had taken all her control not to look at him for the past couple of hours, though she knew he hadn't taken his eyes off her. She'd felt his gaze through every greeting, every new reader, every conversation.

She swallowed but stood her ground, hating the way she devoured the sight of him. The way her pulse quickened as familiar excitement stroked her. She was famished for the sight and sound of him. For his touch, his warm, spicy scent.

'We need to speak. Let's go somewhere private.'

She shook her head. They were in clear view of anyone walking by and that suited her. Being alone with him could only bring more heartache.

'There's nothing more to say, Fotis.'

Despite the passers-by, they were out of earshot, if they kept their voices low. Carlotta hovered several metres away, talking to one of the staff, darting concerned glances. Bless the woman for wanting to protect her, but she could handle this.

'I need to talk with you alone. It's important.' His voice was a velvet rumble that threatened her resolve.

'This is as alone as we get. If that doesn't suit, there's somewhere else I need to be.' She reached for her bag.

'Congratulations on your success, Rosa. I'm happy you stepped out of the shadows and claimed your place. That took a lot of courage.'

'Thank you.' Later she'd appreciate those words. For now, it was agony being close to him. She had to escape. She turned away.

'There's something else, Rosa.'

To her deep despair, the way he said her name still undid her. Tense muscles loosened and her insides unravelled.

'No! There's nothing. You think I don't know the so-called publishing assistant over there is a bodyguard? Or that you arranged for others? I know you have strong protective instincts but I'm not your responsibility.' She saw his lips part, knew he'd argue, and couldn't bear it. 'I don't want a *minder*,' she snapped, whipping up anger as a defence. 'I want a *man*. One who's strong enough to believe in himself and in me. Now, it's time I left.'

She'd taken a step away when a single word stopped her. 'Please.'

She froze, hearing something in that one syllable she'd never heard from Fotis. Desperation. Longing. Something more, so powerful she drew the sound deep inside, holding it, afraid of what would happen if she let it go.

'You're absolutely right.' His voice was hoarse, as if his throat had constricted like hers. She was sure hers was lined with sandpaper. 'You deserve so much more than I offered. I'm ashamed, Rosa. I was a coward, all the time telling myself I was doing the right thing, pushing you away to protect you from even worse hurt, but all the while I was protecting myself.'

Slowly she turned back. Beyond him everything was a blur. All she saw was him, hands open by his sides, wearing an expression of such pain that answering grief stoppered her throat.

How could a man with such innate strength look suddenly so gaunt? Haunted? His cheeks hollowed, those bright eyes dimming as if he were a shadow of the person she knew. It killed her to see him that way.

'I came to say you were right. About me. I've been scared since I was a boy, scared of caring too much and losing what I cared for. Terrified of connecting, much less loving.' His chest rose on a deep breath and she saw a pulse race at his temple. 'It was easier to cut myself off. But I did yearn for more. For community. Friends. Love.'

His words reverberated between them, dying away into thickening silence.

She'd been hurt too many times. It had taken all her strength to walk away last time and now...

Rosamund shook her head, torn between excitement and fear. Her flesh was cold but scorching heat radiated inside. She blinked as fire burned the back of her eyes.

Instantly Fotis was there, so close she had to angle her head up to hold his gaze. And suddenly there was fire in his eyes too, blazing down at her, holding her in thrall. He might be haunted by past pain, but he was strong, a survivor, willing to learn from his mistakes.

'I was terrified, Rosa, because with you I wanted everything. I wanted us to continue as we were but I wanted so much more, things I'd never considered. I want you body and soul. I want to laugh with you, share with you, build a future with you.'

His words stole the air from her lungs, because she could see, feel, that he meant every syllable. The air crackled between them, her fingertips tingled as hope ghosted along her spine and settled near her heart. When he spoke like that...

But this time caution, the product of past hurts, stopped her. 'I...' She shook her head.

'It's all right, *asteri mou*. I know I'm another man who let you down when you deserved better. I know you need time to think. I won't crowd you.'

He raised his hands and stepped back. Part of Rosamund went with him.

'I love you, Rosa.'

Again her heart seemed to stop, before taking up a rackety, excited beat. Had she heard him right?

'I didn't know it at the time, but I suspect I loved you from the moment you went toe-to-toe with me that day in Paris, when you put me in my place then strutted off the plane. But what I feel for you is deeper than attraction. It's something I'll carry all my life, whether you forgive me or not.'

He smiled then, a rare, crooked smile that hooked her heart.

Who was she kidding? Her heart had been hooked from the first.

'You need space,' he said. 'I respect that. I'll go now and—'

'You're not going anywhere.'

One winged eyebrow rose. 'I'm not?'

'If you loved me, would you really go back to Greece now?'

'Who said anything about Greece? I'm trying to be reasonable, not pressure you. I've booked a suite in your hotel. I'm going to invite you to breakfast tomorrow when you've had time to think. I'm going to work on convincing you to forgive me, then I'm going to woo you properly.'

So, far from accepting defeat and retreating, he had a plan to coax her out from behind her defences. Or wear her down. Or perhaps seduce her into changing her mind. Anticipation rippled across her skin and eddied in her womb.

That was the man she'd fallen for. Powerful, clever, single-minded.

It was just as well she loved him the way he was.

Despite the gravity of the moment, her mouth twitched. 'Wooing? That sounds very old-fashioned.'

His eyes narrowed as if he read her changing emotions. 'My intentions are of the old-fashioned variety. I want to marry you, Rosa.'

Shock compounded on shock, but somehow each one was easier to take. She was learning to like the surprises Fotis offered today. Love. Wooing. A future together.

From the corner of her eye she saw heads turn in their direction. They'd forgotten to keep their voices down. She didn't care, and nor did Fotis, given his expression.

Nevertheless, she stepped closer, close enough to slip her hands beneath his jacket and plant them on his solid chest. The steady throb of his heart eased the last ache in her chest.

'Yes, please. I still love you, Fotis. I always will.'

His arms went around her, pulling her in as he groaned deep in his throat and kissed the top of her head then peppered kisses over her face. 'I don't deserve you, Rosa. I was petrified you'd changed your mind.'

'Never,' she whispered as she lifted her mouth to his. 'I want to spend my life with you. I've been so miserable—'

'Sh, *asteri mou*. I was a blind idiot but I'm going to make it up to you. We're going to be so happy.'

She slid her hands up to clasp the back of his neck, luxuriating in how good they felt together. In the impossible excitement of knowing this was only the beginning. 'I know.'

Then the globe's most reclusive billionaire and the world's most talked-about princess kissed passionately, ignoring the gathering crowd and raised phones.

They were in love and didn't care who knew it.

EPILOGUE

THE HUGE CHRISTMAS TREE twinkled with lights. Rosamund stifled a laugh as her toddler nephew stood at its base, wonderment in his eyes as he looked up to where it almost reached the frescoed ceiling. He craned his neck so far he lost his balance and abruptly sat on the floor, beaming.

'He really is the jolliest little boy,' she murmured, watching her sister-in-law, Susanna, scoop him up and carry him over to Leon.

'You want one like that?' Fotis' voice was like liquid velvet in her ear. His arms came around her, pulling her back against his tall frame, hands possessively smoothing her baby bump.

She sighed and relaxed against him. 'A child who laughs more than he cries? That sounds wonderful. But,' she covered one of his big hands with hers, 'whatever our baby's like, I'll love him or her.'

They were so lucky, to have each other and soon, a child. Beneath their joined hands the bub moved and, though she knew it was coincidence, Rosamund couldn't help imagining it was communicating with them.

'Didn't I tell you she'd be a footballer?'

Rosamund shook her head. What was it about men and football? 'He could be a chess player or a mathematician.'

She shivered as Fotis kissed her neck, his words tickling her skin. 'Or a world-famous author.'

'Sorry to intrude.' Leon appeared, comfortably holding the heir to the throne, who grinned and drooled over his jacket. 'But can I borrow you for a few minutes, Fotis? It's about the children's services initiative I'm planning.'

'You'll need to consult Rosa too.'

'I already gave my thoughts when you were out for a run.' She stroked her nephew's soft cheek, overcome by the idea *their* baby would be here soon. She straightened and turned, realising Fotis was thinking the same thing. His expression made her melt. All that tender protectiveness and anticipation. 'Don't be long, you two. I know what you're like when you get your heads together over a project.'

Fotis' slow smile made her wish they'd already had Christmas dinner and were heading to their suite.

'I promise to be back soon.' He kissed her cheek, sending ripples of delight across her skin.

Rosamund moved to the group around the fireplace, chatting with relatives and family friends. Laughter rang out and she turned to see Dimitria Politis and Susanna's younger brother grinning together. Old Mr Politis was deep in discussion with Rosamund's elderly second cousin. Knowing both, they were either righting the world's wrongs or planning a new business venture.

Fotis and Tassos had spent ages planning a fireworks display back in Greece to see in the new year. Her family—her *family*!—would all travel from Cardona to Greece after Christmas and stay with them over New Year's to share the celebration.

How things had changed.

Her sister-in-law stopped beside her. 'What are you looking so happy about? Might it have something to do with a fascinating, dark-haired Greek?'

Rosamund shrugged. 'What can I say? I'm a lucky woman.'

'We both are.' Susanna slipped her arm through Rosamund's. 'I'm so glad you and Leon are spending more time together. That means you and *I* get time together too.'

Rosamund leaned closer, smiling at the glow of belonging she felt. 'I feel the same.' Leon's wife was a wonderful woman. 'I was just thinking how much fun it is to have two family celebrations. Did I mention there'll be a huge fireworks display on the island?'

Susanna looked past her, eyes dancing. 'I don't think you'll have to wait until next week for fireworks.' She slipped her arm free. 'I'd better check the meal's ready. But...' Her voice turned mock-stern, 'don't go getting distracted.'

She strode off, just as a warm hand captured Rosamund's. 'Have I told you, *asteri mou*, that you look gorgeous in silver? No other woman holds a candle to you.'

She grinned and cupped Fotis' jaw in her palms. 'You have, but I never tire of hearing it.'

'Excellent.' His head dipped, gaze fixed on her mouth.

A voice announced, 'Dinner is served.' Seconds later Susanna murmured beside them, 'That includes you two.'

Fotis lifted his head, mock-frowning. 'She's bossy.'

Rosamund pressed a quick kiss to his lips. 'Just as well you like strong women.'

He threaded his fingers through hers. 'Absolutely. And you like challenging men.'

They shared a secret smile then turned and followed their family into the dining room, hands linked and hearts full.

* * * * *

Did you fall head over heels for
Forbidden Princess's Billionaire Bodyguard?
Then you're certain to love these other intensely emotional stories from Annie West!

Signed, Sealed, Married
Unknown Royal Baby
Ring for an Heir
Queen by Royal Command
Stolen Pregnant Bride

Available now!

Get up to 4 Free Books!

We'll send you 2 free books from each series you try PLUS a free Mystery Gift.

FREE Value Over **$25**

Both the **Harlequin Presents** and **Harlequin Medical Romance** series feature exciting stories of passion and drama.

YES! Please send me 2 FREE novels from Harlequin Presents or Harlequin Medical Romance and my FREE gift (gift is worth about $10 retail). After receiving them, if I don't wish to receive any more books, I can return the shipping statement marked "cancel." If I don't cancel, I will receive 6 brand-new larger-print novels every month and be billed just $7.19 each in the U.S., or $7.99 each in Canada, or 4 brand-new Harlequin Medical Romance Larger-Print books every month and be billed just $7.19 each in the U.S. or $7.99 each in Canada, a savings of 20% off the cover price. It's quite a bargain! Shipping and handling is just 50¢ per book in the U.S. and $1.25 per book in Canada.* I understand that accepting the 2 free books and gift places me under no obligation to buy anything. I can always return a shipment and cancel at any time. The free books and gift are mine to keep no matter what I decide.

Choose one:
- ☐ **Harlequin Presents Larger-Print** (176/376 BPA G36Y)
- ☐ **Harlequin Medical Romance** (171/371 BPA G36Y)
- ☐ **Or Try Both!** (176/376 & 171/371 BPA G36Z)

Name (please print)

Address   Apt. #

City   State/Province   Zip/Postal Code

Email: Please check this box ☐ if you would like to receive newsletters and promotional emails from Harlequin Enterprises ULC and its affiliates. You can unsubscribe anytime.

Mail to the Harlequin Reader Service:
IN U.S.A.: P.O. Box 1341, Buffalo, NY 14240-8531
IN CANADA: P.O. Box 603, Fort Erie, Ontario L2A 5X3

Want to explore our other series or interested in ebooks? Visit www.ReaderService.com or call 1-800-873-8635.

---

*Terms and prices subject to change without notice. Prices do not include sales taxes, which will be charged (if applicable) based on your state or country of residence. Canadian residents will be charged applicable taxes. Offer not valid in Quebec. This offer is limited to one order per household. Books received may not be as shown. Not valid for current subscribers to the Harlequin Presents or Harlequin Medical Romance series. All orders subject to approval. Credit or debit balances in a customer's account(s) may be offset by any other outstanding balance owed by or to the customer. Please allow 4 to 6 weeks for delivery. Offer available while quantities last.

Your Privacy—Your information is being collected by Harlequin Enterprises ULC, operating as Harlequin Reader Service. For a complete summary of the information we collect, how we use this information and to whom it is disclosed, please visit our privacy notice located at https://corporate.harlequin.com/privacy-notice. Notice to California Residents – Under California law, you have specific rights to control and access your data. For more information on these rights and how to exercise them, visit https://corporate.harlequin.com/california-privacy. For additional information for residents of other U.S. states that provide their residents with certain rights with respect to personal data, visit https://corporate.harlequin.com/other-state-residents-privacy-rights/.

HPHM25